# FRIENDLY WARNING

BEN COWAN GOT to his feet. "Bijah . . . this is government business if you cross the line into Mexico. It's up to me to stop you."

Catlow grinned at him. "Stop me, then. But I'd still like to have you in with me."

Ben put on his hat. "Sorry I can't talk you out of this, but I didn't much figure I could." He put out his hand. "We'll meet again."

"You keep your ears pinned back when we do, or I'll notch 'em for you. This is the big one for me, Ben, an' all bets are off."

Ben Cowan stepped out into the night. . . .

# Bantam Books by Louis L'Amour

**NOVELS**

Bendigo Shafter
Borden Chantry
Brionne
The Broken Gun
The Burning Hills
The Californios
Callaghen
Catlow
Chancy
The Cherokee Trail
Comstock Lode
Conagher
Crossfire Trail
Dark Canyon
Down the Long Hills
The Empty Land
Fair Blows the Wind
Fallon
The Ferguson Rifle
The First Fast Draw
Flint
Guns of the Timberlands
Hanging Woman Creek
The Haunted Mesa
Heller with a Gun
The High Graders
High Lonesome
Hondo
How the West Was Won
The Iron Marshal
The Key-Lock Man
Kid Rodelo
Kilkenny
Killoe
Kilrone
Kiowa Trail
Last of the Breed
Last Stand at Papago
  Wells
The Lonesome Gods
The Man Called Noon
The Man from Skibbereen
The Man from the Broken
  Hills
Matagorda
Milo Talon
The Mountain Valley War
North to the Rails
Over on the Dry Side
Passin' Through
The Proving Trail

The Quick and the Dead
Radigan
Reilly's Luck
The Rider of Lost Creek
Rivers West
The Shadow Riders
Shalako
Showdown at Yellow
  Butte
Silver Canyon
Sitka
Son of a Wanted Man
Taggart
The Tall Stranger
To Tame a Land
Tucker
Under the Sweetwater Rim
Utah Blaine
The Walking Drum
Westward the Tide
Where the Long Grass
  Blows

**SHORT STORY
COLLECTIONS**

Beyond the Great Snow
  Mountains
Bowdrie
Bowdrie's Law
Buckskin Run
The Collected Short Sto-
  ries of Louis L'Amour
  (vols. 1–7)
Dutchman's Flat
End of the Drive
From the Listening Hills
The Hills of Homicide
Law of the Desert Born
Long Ride Home
Lonigan
May There Be a Road
Monument Rock
Night over the Solomons
Off the Mangrove Coast
The Outlaws of Mesquite
The Rider of the Ruby
  Hills
Riding for the Brand
The Strong Shall Live
The Trail to Crazy Man
Valley of the Sun
War Party

West from Singapore
West of Dodge
With These Hands
Yondering

**SACKETT TITLES**

Sackett's Land
To the Far Blue
  Mountains
The Warrior's Path
Jubal Sackett
Ride the River
The Daybreakers
Sackett
Lando
Mojave Crossing
Mustang Man
The Lonely Men
Galloway
Treasure Mountain
Lonely on the Mountain
Ride the Dark Trail
The Sackett Brand
The Sky-Liners

**THE HOPALONG CASSIDY
NOVELS**

The Riders of High Rock
The Rustlers of West Fork
The Trail to Seven Pines
Trouble Shooter

**NONFICTION**

Education of a
  Wandering Man
Frontier
The Sackett Companion:
  A Personal Guide to
  the Sackett Novels
A Trail of Memories:
  The Quotations of
  Louis L'Amour,
  compiled by
  Angelique L'Amour

**POETRY**

Smoke from This Altar

**LOST TREASURES**

Louis L'Amour's Lost
  Treasures: Volume 1

# CATLOW

A NOVEL

## Louis L'Amour

Postscript by Beau L'Amour

BANTAM BOOKS

NEW YORK

*Catlow* is a work of fiction. Names, characters, places,
and incidents are the products of the author's imagination
or are used fictitiously. Any resemblance to actual events, locales,
or persons, living or dead, is entirely coincidental.

2018 Bantam Books Mass Market Edition

Copyright © 1963 by Louis & Katherine L'Amour Trust
Postscript by Beau L'Amour copyright © 2018 by Beau L'Amour

Published in the United States by Bantam Books,
an imprint of Random House, a division of
Penguin Random House LLC, New York.

BANTAM and the HOUSE colophon are registered trademarks of
Penguin Random House LLC.

Originally published in the United States by Bantam Books,
an imprint of Random House, a division of
Penguin Random House LLC, in 1963.

ISBN 978-0-525-48626-8
ebook ISBN 978-0-525-48634-3

Cover art: Frank McCarthy

Printed in the United States of America

randomhousebooks.com

9  8  7  6  5  4  3  2  1

Bantam Books mass market edition: May 2018

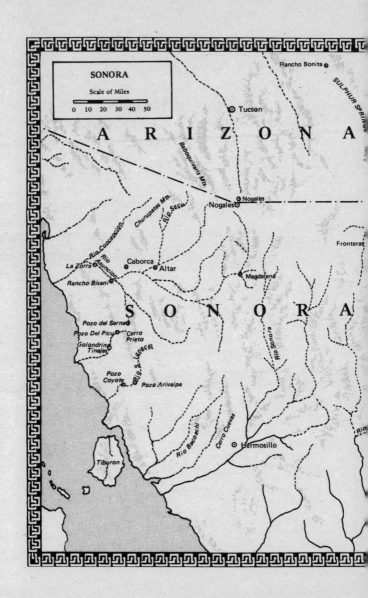

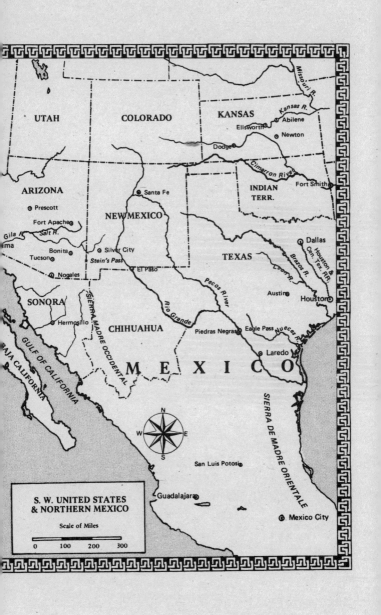

S. W. UNITED STATES
& NORTHERN MEXICO

Scale of Miles

0     100    200    300

# CHAPTER 1

WHEREVER BUFFALO GRAZED, cattle were rounded up, or mustangs tossed their tails in flight, men talked of Bijah Catlow.

He was a brush-buster from the *brazada* country down along the Nueces, and he could ride anything that wore hair. He made his brag that he could out-fight, outride, outtalk, and outlove any man in the world, and he was prepared to accept challenges, any time or place.

Around chuck-wagon fires or line camps from the Brazos to the Musselshell, men talked of Bijah Catlow. They talked of his riding, his shooting, or the wild brawls in which, no matter how angry others became, Bijah never lost his temper—or the fight.

Abijah was his name, shortened in the manner of the frontier to Bijah. He was a broad-shouldered, deep-chested, hell-for-leather Irishman who emerged from the War Between the States with three decorations for bravery, three courts-martial, and a reputation for being a man to have on your side in any kind of a shindig, brannigan, or plain old alley fight.

A shock-headed man with a disposition as open as a Panhandle prairie, he was as ready to fight as an Irishman at a Dutchman's picnic; and where the wishes of Bijah Catlow were crossed he recognized the laws of neither God nor man. But the law had occasion to recognize Bijah Catlow; and the law knew him best in the person of Marshal Ben Cowan.

By the time Bijah and Ben were fifteen years old, each had saved the other's life no less than three times; and Bijah had whipped Ben four times and had himself been whipped four times. Ben was tough, good-humored, and serious; Bijah was tough, good-humored, and wild as any unbroken mustang.

At nineteen, Ben Cowan was a deputy sheriff, and at twenty-three a Deputy United States Marshal. By the time Bijah had reached the age of twenty-three he was a known cattle rustler, and an outlaw with three killings behind him.

But it was no criminal instinct, inherited or acquired, that turned Bijah from the paths of righteousness to the shadowy trails of crime. It was a simple matter of frontier economics.

Bijah Catlow was a top-hand in any man's outfit, so when he signed on with the Tumbling SS's it was no reflection on his riding. He hired out at the going wage of thirty dollars per month and found, but the sudden demand for beef at the Kansas railheads turned Texas longhorns from unwanted, unsought wild creatures into a means to wealth and affluence.

From occasional drives to Missouri, Louisiana, or even Illinois, or the casual slaughter of cattle for their hides, the demand for beef in the eastern cities lifted the price per head to ten or more times its former value.

Immediately the big ranchers offered a bonus of two dollars per head for every maverick branded, and Bijah Catlow, who worked with all the wholehearted enthusiasm with which he played, plunged into the business of branding cattle to get rich.

He was a brush-popper and a good one, and he knew where the wild cattle lurked. He was a good hand with a rope and he owned some fast horses that knew cattle as well as he did, and nobody knew them better. The first month after the bonus was initiated, Bijah Catlow roped and slapped an iron on eighty-seven head of wild cattle.

During the months that followed, Bijah was busier than a man with a dollar watch and the seven-year itch (when he isn't winding, he's scratching) and he averaged two hundred to two hundred fifty dollars a month. In those days nobody made that kind of money on the range, or much of anywhere else. And then the bottom dropped out.

The owners of the big brands got together and agreed that the bonus was foolish and unnecessary, for it was the hands' job to brand cattle anyhow. So the bonus came to an end.

From comparative affluence, Bijah Catlow once again became a thirty-a-month cowhand, and he led the contingent that quit abruptly.

His argument was a good one. Why brand cattle for the ranchers? Why not for themselves? Why not make up their own herd and drive through to Kansas?

After all, most of the mavericks running loose on the plains of Texas came from Lord knew where, for cattle had been breeding like jackrabbits on those plains ever since the days when the first Spanish came there. Nobody could claim or had claimed ownership of those cattle until suddenly they became valuable. Moreover, throughout the War Between the States most of the riders had been away at war and the cattle that might have been branded had gone maverick, and many of their owners had never returned from the War.

The cattle were there for whoever claimed them—so Bijah Catlow banded together a group of riders like himself and they went to work, inspired by Bijah's wholehearted zeal and unflagging energy.

He threw himself into the work with the same enthusiasm with which he did everything else, and it was his zest that fired the ambition of the others. Morning, noon, and night they worked, and at the end of two months they had a herd of nearly three thousand head ready for the trail.

Wild cattle were plentiful in those early years, and the smoke of their branding fires was forever in the air. The riders plunged into the deepest brush and rousted out old mossyhorns and branded them for the Kansas trail, but their work did not go untroubled. Twice they drove off raiding Comanches, and Nigger Jim was gored by an angry bull. They found his ruined body sprawled in the grass near a tiny seep, the earth around torn by the furious battle. A swarthy man, part Indian rather than Negro, he had been a top-hand and a good companion. They buried him on the prairie where they found him.

A few days later Johnny Caxton lost an arm. He was snubbing a rope to a tree, and how it happened he never knew. The plunging steer wheeled suddenly and Caxton's arm was caught in a loop of the rope. The steer lunged back on the rope and it snapped tight around Johnny Caxton's arm.

Two days before he had lost his holster in the

brush when it was torn from his belt, and although he had found his pistol, he had been carrying it in his saddlebag since then. His horse was some distance off, and he had been stalking the big steer afoot when he got his chance to make the throw.

It was hours before they found him, the tough old mossyhorn still backed to the end of the rope, full of fight and glaring wild-eyed, and Johnny sagging against the tree, his arm a black and ugly sight.

There was no doctor within a hundred miles, so Bijah Catlow amputated the arm in camp, cauterizing the stump with a hot branding iron.

It was a week later, with four of their number a quarter of a mile away riding herd on the cattle, that Bijah awakened to find their camp surrounded.

The first man he saw was Sheriff Jack Mercer, formerly on the payroll of Parkman of the OP Bar, and now, as sheriff, reputed to be still on his payroll. Then he saw Parkman himself, Barney Staples of the Tumbling SS, and Osgood of the Three Links. With them were twenty-odd tough cowhands who rode for their brands.

Neither Sheriff Mercer or Parkman had ever liked Bijah Catlow. A year before, when Mercer was still a cowhand, Catlow had whipped him unmercifully in a brawl, and Parkman hated Catlow because the cowhand could get a girl that Parkman could not.

Bijah, who was no fool, knew he was in trouble. Glancing around as he sat up and tugged on his boots, he saw no friendly faces. He had worked for Staples and always turned in a good job, but Staples was a cattleman and would stand with the rest.

Mercer leaned his big hands on the pommel of his

saddle. Deep within him the fire of triumph burned with a hard, evil flame. "Bijah," he said, "I've got a bronc I say you can't ride. Not if you meet the conditions."

Bijah Catlow was not sure how much they wanted the others, but he knew they wanted him. "What's the matter, boys?" he said. "Why the visit?"

"You're a damned, no-good cow rustler," Parkman said. "We hang rustlers."

"Turn the rest of these boys loose," Bijah said, "and I'll ride your bronc—whatever the conditions."

"You ain't heard the conditions," Mercer said. "You ride him with your hands tied behind your back and your neck in a noose . . . under that cottonwood over there."

Bijah Catlow got easily to his feet and stamped into his boots. He was wearing his gun . . . it was always the first thing he put on after his hat . . . and he had already put both hat and gun on when he got up to stir the fire, half an hour before. Nobody had told him to drop his belt. After all, three of them had guns on them.

On his own side, Rio Bray was there, and Bob Keleher—and Johnny Caxton, of course. Since his arm had been lost Johnny had taken over the job of camp roustabout, rustling firewood and water for whoever was cooking for the day. They were good men, but Caxton had lost his right arm and still hadn't won much use of his left, although he had been working on it every day.

"You let them go," Bijah said, "and I'll ride your damned horse."

Mercer's smile was one of contempt. "You'll do

what we tell you . . . and all of you will get a chance at that same bronc."

Bijah thought for a moment that Staples was going to object, but he did not. After all, it was Parkman who was top man here. Bijah knew that when he went for his gun.

Nobody expected it, although they all should have, knowing Bijah Catlow.

Rio Bray probably guessed it first, for as Bijah's gun came up shooting, Rio dove for the shotgun that lay across his saddle. Rio hit the ground, rolled over, and came up on his belly with the shotgun in his hands, and the first thing he saw was Parkman pulling leather on a plunging horse, blood on his shirt front, and Jack Mercer falling.

Rio fired one barrel, then another, and two saddles emptied.

The shooting and the plunging of Parkman's horse destroyed any chance they had at the small targets that faced them in the Catlow camp. And about that time Old Man Merridew, who had been out with the cattle, cut loose with a Sharps fifty.

The cattlemen's posse stampeded and left Jack Mercer dead on the ground. Parkman managed to cling to his saddle and his horse fled with the others.

They were not scared. They were a hard-bitten lot of old Indian fighters, that posse. But they also knew that Old Man Merridew was behind that Sharps buffalo gun, and Merridew was a man who seldom missed what he shot at. It was wide-open prairie where they were, and Merridew was in a tiny hollow of rocks and brush on top of a knoll.

Besides, Bijah Catlow had a gun in his hand, and nobody was buying that if there was a way out.

There was a way, and they took it. After all, they could always get Bijah Catlow. He wasn't going any place.

The law in that section of Texas was whatever the big cattle outfits said it was, and the law said Bijah Catlow was a rustler and a killer. He had killed an officer in performance of his duty, and he became a wanted man.

---

WHEN PARKMAN BECAME conscious in the big four-poster in his own ranch house he issued the order: "Get Bijah Catlow."

There was a good deal of sympathy in the room for Catlow, but nobody spoke up. To do so was to invite ruin.

Ben Cowan was not present. He was not even in the state at the time. Had he been, he might have told them not to count their hangings until they had a neck in the noose. Somebody had said that Catlow was not going any place . . . Cowan would have looked his disgust at that. He would have known that Bijah Catlow was already gone.

Within the hour the herd was moving over the river, three miles to the north. They drove on through the night and finally bedded the herd down two hours after daybreak on a small branch far west of the Kansas trail.

By noon they were moving again, following the trail north that had been made by a herd of buffalo, losing their own tracks in the wider trail of the big herd.

Bijah glanced to the south. "Hope there's another herd coming along to wipe out whatever sign we leave," he commented, "because Parkman will be along."

Old Man Merridew lifted a skinny arm and pointed it the way his hawk-beak nose was already pointing. "They's a-comin'," he said. "There's the dust!"

"Maybe that's the posse," Bray suggested.

Merridew spat. "Them's buffler," he said. "Maybe eight, ten thousand of them . . . maybe more."

Nobody argued with Old Man. He had eyes better than any eagle, and a nose to smell buffalo as far as a man could see. The Old Man was older than anybody knew, and looked old enough in the face to have worn out three bodies . . . but he was wiry, strong, and tough as any old Cheyenne or Comanche.

North they drove, with the Drinking Gourd hanging in the sky before them.

North they rode, and Bijah Catlow, the flamboyant, good-natured, hell-for-leather Bijah had become an outlaw.

It would be another week before Ben Cowan heard the news.

# CHAPTER 2

DEPUTY UNITED STATES Marshal Ben Cowan was having troubles of his own. He was deep into the Cross Timbers, trailing a bad Indian.

The Tonkawa Kid was no blanket Indian, but an occasional cowhand, farm laborer, and horse trader who had turned renegade. Exactly a month before he had killed and robbed a farmer in the Cherokee Nation, attacked and murdered the farmer's wife, and killed a neighbor attracted by the shooting. Unfortunately for the Tonkawa Kid, the neighbor lived long enough to identify him.

This was the fourth such crime in the vicinity within the year, and then somebody remembered that Tonkawa had been spending more money than he had earned. A sorrel mare he traded in Fort Smith had been stolen from the scene of one of the earlier murders.

Ben Cowan's canteen was dry, and he was working his way toward the Cimarron, hoping to find some branch flowing into the river where he could get water. The river itself was a last resort, for at this season of the year, in this area it was too thick to drink, too thin to plow.

The Cross Timbers country was hell's borderland. It was a stubby forest of blackjack and post-oak mixed with occasional patches of prickly pear. Along the few small streams, most of them intermittent, were redbud, persimmon, and dogwood. Here and there were open meadows, varying in extent. In places the forest was practically impenetrable.

Blackjack, a kind of scrub oak, had a way of sending roots out just under the surface, and at various distances new trees would spring up from these roots. The result was a series of dense thickets, the earth beneath them matted with roots, their stiff branches intermingled.

There were trails made by wild horses and occasional small herds of buffalo or deer, and these usually led from meadow to meadow across the vast stretch of country covered by the Cross Timbers.

It was the spring of the year and the blackjack still held many of the past season's leaves, brown and stiff. Only along the occasional streams was there beauty, this provided by the redbud which grew in thick clumps, its dark, beautiful branches covered with tiny magenta-colored blossoms.

Except in the meadows, grass was scarce. Under the blackjacks there were thick carpets of matted leaves that seemed to crackle at the slightest touch.

It was hot and still. On a branch not far ahead a cardinal peered at something in the grass, and Ben Cowan drew up.

The bright crimson of the bird was a brilliant touch of color in the drab surroundings, but Ben Cowan had reason to be wary. A man in the wilderness soon learns to pay strict attention to the information that birds and animals can give him, and this bird was watching something he did not like.

The last officer out of Fort Smith who had trailed an Indian outlaw into the Cross Timbers had been found with a bullet through his skull, which for added effect had been bashed in after he had fallen.

Ben Cowan snaked his Winchester from the scabbard, and waited uneasily. Bees droned nearby in the still air. Sweat trickled down his face, prickly with dust. He listened, squinting his eyes against the salt sting of the sweat.

It was dreadfully hot where he sat his horse, and he desperately wished to move. The situation was not at all good, for there was only one direction in which he could go without turning back, and that was straight ahead. Off to the left beyond a thick patch of blackjack there seemed to be a clearing or meadow.

A fly buzzed annoyingly around his face, and he inadvertently lifted a hand to brush it away. Instantly a bullet thudded into the trunk of a tree near his face, spattering him with a hail of tiny fragments. Momentarily blinded by them, he fell from the saddle.

He did it without thinking. It was one of those instinctively right reactions that come to a fighting man who is constantly aware and alert. The position of his horse was such that quick escape was impossible, but there was space to fall in, so he fell.

He hit the ground and rolled over, then lay still. Fortunately, he had retained his grip on his Winchester. Now he put it on the ground and pawed at his eyes, frightened by the thought of being blinded with an enemy so close by.

That enemy had to be close. There was nowhere around where a man could see over thirty or forty yards at most, and even at that distance a shot was a chancy thing, with all the intermingled branches that might deflect the bullet.

Still feeling a few tiny particles in his eyes, Ben Cowan took up his Winchester and turned his eyes this way and that to locate himself.

He had fallen into a shallow depression, only inches below the level of the forest floor. Where he lay there was a small patch of dead brown grass. Right before his head rose the trunk of the tree, not over eight inches in diameter, from which he had received the shower of bark. To his left there was a deadfall and the stark white skeleton of a lightning-shattered tree.

He lay very still. His head was in the shade, but the sun was hot upon his back. In a low-growing black-jack close by, he saw a blacksnake writhing in sinuous coils among the branches. The snake stopped moving and was still.

The Tonkawa Kid, he recalled, had several renegade cousins, and was reputed to travel with them on occasion. It might be there was more than one man lying in wait for a shot at him.

Ben Cowan was a patient man. Tall, lean, and handsome in a rugged way, he was inclined to be methodical. He was a painstaking man, without making any great issue of it. Bijah Catlow had often said that nobody, anywhere, could track better than Ben Cowan, and he might well have added that he never had met anybody who could punch harder. There was a thickening in Bijah's left ear that had resulted from one of Cowan's blows; and the faintly discernible hump in Cowan's nose marked where Bijah had broken it.

But Ben Cowan was not thinking of Bijah Catlow now. He was thinking of the Tonkawa Kid.

That Indian, wily as any fox and slippery as any snake, was somewhere close by, and even now might be working his way into position to kill him, yet Cowan could do nothing. To move silently with those stiff, crackling blackjack leaves lying about was virtually impossible—or was it?

Off to his right a blue jay started raising a fuss . . . something was worrying it. The sounds the jay made were not unlike those it made when it saw a snake, but different, too. Ben Cowan slid his rifle forward a bit and, easing over on his left shoulder, he looked up into the tree above him.

The tree was actually one of two twin trees of about equal size, and the limbs grew low. There was a fair-sized branch, a relatively wide space, then another branch, and more above; the other twin leaned close up higher, the branches interwoven. It was a risk, but if he could pull himself up there . . . His clothing was non-descript as to color and it might blend well with the tree and the scattered leaves that remained.

He studied the branches. A grasp there, a quick pull-up, a foot there, then another pull-up, avoiding those leaves.

Carefully, he lifted himself to his knees, cringing against the half-expected impact of a bullet, then he straightened to his feet, grasped the branch and pulled himself up. He got his boot on a lower branch, and then moved up again.

Not the brush of a leaf or the scrape of a boot, and he was there. His eyes searched the trees, the grass, the brush. What he saw was brown grass springing back into position only a few yards away. He looked into the brush . . . a faint stir of movement and he glimpsed the Tonkawa. Instantly, he fired.

And in the same instant he knew he had been suckered into a trap.

Another bullet spattered bark in his face and something struck his leg a wicked blow and knocked it from its perch. He fell, with the sound of other bullets echoing in his ears. A branch broke as his body hit it, and then he struck the ground with a thud. His horse leaped away, blowing with fear, and Ben Cowan heard the rush of feet in the grass.

He had lost his grip on his rifle and he clawed wildly for his six-shooter, coming up with it just as an Indian broke through the brush, gun in hand, eyes distended with excitement.

Ben Cowan triggered the .45 . . . he fired upward, firing quickly and aiming, he thought, for the Indian's broad chest. The bullet was high, striking the man's chin and smashing upward, driving a bloody furrow along his chin, tearing his nose away, and entering the skull at the top of the eye socket.

Cowan whirled, felt a bullet burn his cheek, and fired blindly at a leaping shadow. The shadow broke stride and fell, the Indian dead before he hit the ground.

Two down . . . how many were there? Neither of them was the Tonkawa Kid.

Ben Cowan twisted around, found his rifle, and pulled himself to it. His leg felt numb, and when he put his hand up to his cheek it came away bloody . . . a bullet had grazed the cheekbone.

He eased himself back into a better defensive position and, reaching out with his rifle, tried to draw the rifle of one of the Tonks a bit closer.

The forest was silent again. He gripped the other rifle, put it close at hand, and then with care ejected the empty shells from his pistol and reloaded.

Nothing happened. The slow minutes passed and Ben Cowan suddenly felt sick and weak. His leg was throbbing. Gingerly, he reached down and felt of the leg. The bullet had cut through the muscle of the calf, and his pants leg and sock were soaked with blood. He must get that boot off and get his leg bandaged . . . but somewhere around was the Tonkawa . . . perhaps more than one.

Delicately, he began to work at the boot to get it off, trying to make no sound. After a few minutes he did get it off, and removed the blood-soaked sock.

His horse, frightened by the shooting, had disappeared, and with it whatever he had, which was little enough, to treat his wound. So he packed grass around it and tied it with his handkerchief, then struggled into his boot. At intervals, he paused to listen.

By this time the Kid undoubtedly knew his friends had run into trouble, if he had not actually seen what happened. Hence, he was either going to run or wait and try again; and if Ben Cowan was any judge, the Kid would wait and take his chance.

His eyes seemed to mist over, and when he tried to move he felt a sudden weakness.

Suppose he passed out? It was possible, for he had lost a lot of blood. If he did pass out, he would be killed.

He must hide.

Somehow, in some way, he must hide. Carefully, he looked about him, but there was nowhere to hide. Only the clumped blackjack, the black trunks of the trees.

But he had to move. He could no longer remain here—if he passed out where he was he would get his throat cut while unconscious. Far better to take his chances in trying to do something.

The nearest Indian had been carrying a Winchester also, so he stripped the man's cartridge belt from him, and his knife. Then he eased from behind the tree and began inching his way through the grass.

He succeeded in moving without making any noise but the slightest dragging sound . . . that was inevitable. But, it was less than he had expected, and at times he even made no noise at all. His eyes continually searched the ground, the trees, the shrubs. He had gone at least thirty yards when he heard a chuckle.

It was the faintest of sounds, but he froze in place, listening. After a minute, he started on.

"Go ahead," a voice said, "you ain't goin' no place."

The voice was harsh and ugly. It was the Tonkawa Kid. Ben Cowan could not see him, but he knew the Kid must be where he could watch Cowan. Where was that?

He pulled himself a little farther along, sorting the places in his mind. When the Kid spoke again, Cowan threw his rifle around and fired at the sound.

From a few feet away, the Kid laughed again, and fired. A bullet tore a furrow in the grass just ahead of Ben Cowan, almost burning his finger. And then he saw the gully that lay only a few feet ahead and to his right. That gully was only inches deep, but it was enough to offer shelter. Moreover, it deepened farther along.

Using his rifle, Ben Cowan suddenly pushed himself up and dove forward. A rifle bellowed behind him even as he fell into the gully. Instantly, despite the tearing pain in his leg, he threw himself farther along and began to scramble to get farther away.

He heard a rush of feet in the grass and wheeled around, throwing his gun up. As the Indian sprang into sight, swinging the gun muzzle down on him, Cowan fired.

At the same instant, from off to the left, there was another gunshot.

The Tonkawa's body was caught in midair by the bullets; it was smashed back and around. Still he tried to bring his gun down on Cowan, but two more bullets ripped into him from the left and he fell into the bottom of the gully, landing only inches from Ben Cowan.

Cowan heard horses walking in the grass, and then a voice singing: *"As I walked out in the streets of Laredo, as I walked out in Laredo one day . . ."*

A horse appeared on the edge of the gully, and a grinning face looked down at him.

It was Bijah Catlow.

# CHAPTER 3

**B**EN COWAN OPENED his eyes and looked up into an evening sky where a few scattered clouds were touched with a faint brushing of rose, and along the horizon a dark fringe of trees shouldered against the coming night.

Something stirred near him, and he turned his head to see Old Man Merridew standing by the fire holding a coffee cup.

"Come out of it, did you? You lost a sight of blood, boy."

"I guess I did."

"You done all right," Merridew acknowledged. "You nailed two of them, and your bullet would have killed the Kid even without ours . . . only maybe not soon enough."

"Where'd you come from?"

"Pushin' a herd to Dodge. Bijah seen your horse, so four, five of us, we left the herd and back-trailed the horse. Figured you to be in some kind of trouble, losin' your mount that way, and your rifle gone.

"Then we heard the shootin', so we closed in kind of careful-like. We found them Tonks you salted down, and one of our boys who used to hang out up in the Nation, he figured it was the Kid you were after. He knowed those Tonks for his kin."

"You came along at the right time."

Merridew shrugged, and filled another cup, then added a dollop of whiskey. He brought it to Cowan. "I dunno . . . you might have made it."

Cowan drank the whiskey and coffee and felt better. "Who are you driving for?"

Merridew glanced up; his hard old eyes were level. "Ourselves . . . who else? When the big outfits dropped the bonus we struck off for ourselves." He looked suspiciously at Cowan. "You mean you ain't heard?"

"That Bijah's wanted for rustling? I heard, but I never believe all I hear. Before I'd believe a thing like that I'd have to hear it from Bijah." He finished the bit of coffee in the bottom of the cup. "As far as I'm concerned, Bijah has as much right to brand mavericks for himself as for the big outfits."

Johnny Caxton rode up to the fire and stepped down from the saddle. Ben Cowan noted the sleeve folded over the stub of the arm, but he offered no comment. When he had last seen Johnny he'd had two good arms, but as far as he was concerned Johnny would be a top-hand under any circumstances.

Johnny glanced his way. "Hi, Ben. Anybody feed you?"

"Just woke up. The Old Man here gave me some special coffee."

Ben Cowan eased his wounded leg out from under the blankets. A thought struck him and he looked quickly around the camp. "You boys missed a day on account of me, didn't you?"

All the signs were there, the question needless. He knew what a camp looked like after a day, and after two days. He also knew how important it was to all of them to get this drive through on time—before Parkman or the law could interfere.

Johnny brought the pot over and refilled his cup. Ben stared bitterly at the coffee. Bijah was a wild one, but he was no thief . . . at least, he never had been. Yet it was a time when many a man was being called an outlaw for slapping brands on cattle. To get away with that, you had to have a big outfit and breeding stock.

"We missed two days," Johnny commented, "one findin' you, one while you're restin' up."

Bijah came in when the guards changed. "Hiya, Shorthorn!" he said. "Surprised somebody hasn't shot that badge off you by now."

He squatted on his heels and studied Ben Cowan with a hard grin. "You packin' a warrant for me?"

"No. If I was, I'd serve it."

Bijah chuckled, and rolled a cigarette. "You ain't changed none." He touched his tongue to the paper. "We goin' to have trouble in Kansas?"

"You know Parkman."

Bijah lighted the cigarette with a stick from the fire. "Nine of us teamed to make this drive, and we rounded up the stock and did the branding. Johnny there, he lost his arm on the job, an' Nigger Jim was killed. Well, Jim left no kin that anybody knows of, but he thought a sight of that girl he was seeing down on the Leon River. Seemed to me we would take his share to her."

Ben Cowan accepted the plate he was handed, and then he said, "Bijah, you drive on to Abilene. When you're a few miles out, I'll ride in and see how things stand."

"I know Bear River Tom Smith," Merridew commented. "He's a reasonable man."

Cowan glanced at him. "Smith's dead. They've brought Wild Bill Hickok in as marshal."

Catlow looked up quickly. "The gunfighter? I've heard of him."

"He's the real thing, and don't forget it," Ben said. "A lot of the boys from down our way underrate him, but don't you make that mistake."

"I'm in too much trouble now," Bijah said. "I'm not riding into Kansas for anything but a chance to sell this herd."

———

NIGHT THREW A shadow on the world, and the night guard looked up from their horses to the circling stars and followed the pointers to the North Star, which was their guide to Kansas. Ben Cowan turned restlessly in his blankets easing his wounded leg against the throbbing pain. He stared up at the stars, reflecting again upon the strange destiny that seemed to tie his life to that of Bijah Catlow.

The thought worried him, for Catlow was a reckless man in many ways—never reckless of his life, although to the casual observer he might seem so, but reckless of the law. But in this case Ben Cowan, like many another Texan, believed Catlow was right, and the branding of mavericks was an old custom.

At dawn they were moving north, Ben Cowan riding his own horse, and easing his leg against the pain.

Bijah dropped back beside him. "Ben, I'm holdin'

them west of the trail, figurin' we ain't so likely to run up against any trouble, that way."

"You duckin' trouble?"

"The boys have got too much at stake. We worked our tails off to get these steers together. Me, I don't care. Neither does the Old Man or Rio Bray; but Johnny, he's got to get him a stake out of this, now that he's left with only one arm."

They rode along a low hill upwind from the herd to stay free of the dust.

"He figures to start him a restaurant," Bijah went on.

"How about you?"

Catlow shot him a quick look. "You goin' to preach at me again? Damn it, Ben, you know I'm pointed for a hangin' or prison, so don't try to head me off."

"You're too good a man, Bijah. Too good to go that way."

"Maybe . . . but I'm a born rebel, Ben. You're the smart one. You'll ride it quiet and come out of it with a sight more than me. I only hope that when the chips are down and they send somebody after me that it won't be you. You wouldn't back up from what you figure is your duty, and I sure wouldn't want you to . . . and I'd never back up, either."

"I know it. I've asked for a transfer to another district, anyway. We may never see each other again."

Bijah slapped him on the shoulder. "That's gloomy talk. I figure to whip your socks off four or five times yet." Bijah threw him a quick glance. "Ben, what you figure to do when we hit Abilene? You said you might help."

"First, I'll clear it with Hickok. He's all right. He doesn't give a damn what happened in Texas or anywhere else. All he wants is peace in Abilene."

"You still have to stack your guns when you come into town?"

"That was under Smith. Wild Bill doesn't care whether you wear them or not, as long as you don't do any shooting. If you decided to do any, you'd better start with him, because if you shoot he'll come after you."

"Smith was a good man. I met up with him that time I rode up to Colorado with that Indian beef." Bijah moved downslope to turn a ranging steer back into the drive. "Why are you so willing to front for me with Wild Bill?"

"He'll listen to me. I'm an officer, too. And you might just be cocky enough to try to throw a gun on him and get killed."

"The way I remember it, you fancy yourself with that hogleg you're carryin'. Why, there was a time you claimed you were faster than me!"

Ben chuckled. "Only said it to you, Bijah, and you know it, you Irish lunkhead. If anybody shoots you, let's keep it in the family."

Catlow laughed good-humoredly. "When the time comes it'll simply bust my heart to kill you. For a sheriff, you're a pretty good sort."

Ben eased his foot in the stirrup, keeping his face straight against the pain. He had no right to complain, with only a bullet through his calf. Johnny Caxton was riding back there with a stump for an arm; but with one arm or two, Johnny Caxton was a good man, and he drove that team of broncs as though he sat the saddle of a bad horse.

Turning in the saddle, Ben Cowan glanced along the herd. Three thousand head of cattle string out for quite a distance when they are not bunched up, and handling this herd was a good big job for the available men. They had about six horses per man, and it wasn't really enough, short-handed as they were.

Ordinarily a herd of three thousand head would have eleven or twelve riders, and the cost was figured at about a dollar-per-head for the drive from Texas to Kansas. In this case, with the herd owned by the drivers, there would be no outlay for wages, and the men owned their own remuda, so there had been no cost for the purchase of horses.

Dawn to dusk they drove, usually trying to water somewhere late in the afternoon, then pushing on a few miles before bedding down. Cattle watered late had a way of starting off better and traveling better than those allowed to water in the morning.

———

ABILENE IN 1871 was a booming town, but the boom was almost over, although few as yet realized it. There were many in town who detested the cattlemen with their vast herds—600,000 head were driven to Abilene that year—and the men who drove them.

Texas Town was wild and woolly, and it was loud. The more staid citizens looked upon it with extreme distaste, and wanted to be rid of the yelling, whooping cowboys, the dusty, trail-seasoned men who were making the town what it was. Only a few months later they were to issue a bulletin saying they wanted no more of it, and to their discomfiture the cattlemen took them at their word and went west to Newton, to Ellsworth, to Dodge. By 1872 the citizens of Abilene were crying for them to come back, but it was too late.

But in 1871 the town was still booming, and Marshal Hickok walked the center of the street, a tall, splendidly built man with auburn hair hanging to his shoulders, his clothing immaculate, his gun always ready for action.

He was the first man Ben Cowan saw when he rode into town.

Hickok had paused on a street corner, glancing each way from the Merchants Hotel. He wore a black frock coat, a low-brimmed black hat, and two ivory-butted and silver-mounted pistols thrust behind a red silk sash.

"Mr. Hickok? I'm Ben Cowan."

Hickok's eyes went from Cowan's eyes to the badge he wore. Hickok held out his hand. "How do you do? What can I do for you?"

Briefly, Cowan explained about Bijah Catlow and the herd. "I know the country down there," Cowan said at the end, "and these cattle were mavericks, open to branding by anyone. I have no share in the business, but Bijah pulled me out of a hole down in the Cross Timbers, and he's a good man."

"We've a letter on the cattle," Hickok replied, "but I am not interested in what happened in Texas.

You tell Catlow to drive his cattle to the stock pens. He won't be bothered unless he or his men make trouble here."

Hickok thrust out his hand again. "Glad to know you, Marshal. We've heard of you."

Ben Cowan limped back to his horse and rode to the Drover's Cottage, where he took a room, and then sat down to write out his report on the case of the Tonkawa Kid. When he had completed it and left it with the mail at the stage station, he went to the telegraph office and wired Fort Smith.

Back at his room he arranged for a bath, and after he had taken it he changed into new clothing bought at Herman Meyer's Clothing Store alongside of the Merchants Hotel.

Bijah Catlow joined him at supper in the dining room at the Drover's Cottage. "Twenty-five dollars a head," Bijah said with a broad smile on his face, "and we split it ten ways, two shares for Johnny Caxton."

He reached into his shirt pocket. "Here's the tally sheet, stamped by the buyer. We picked up a few head of Tumblin' SS's and Ninety-Fours drivin' through, so here's their money. Will you see they get it?"

Ben accepted the money without comment, but offered a receipt. "You're rawhidin' me," Bijah said. "Money in trust to you is safer than any bank."

He looked at Ben, and slowly he began to grin. As he did so he reached for another bit of paper and pushed it across the table. "Stopped by the telegraph office. This is for you."

Ben Cowan opened the folded paper and glanced at it, then he looked up at Bijah. "Did you see this?"

"Sure! I always was too damn' nosey."

Ben glanced down again.

OFFICE OF THE U.S. MARSHAL
FORT SMITH, ARKANSAS.

CONSIDER THIS A WARRANT FOR THE AR-REST OF ABIJAH CATLOW, RIO BRAY, AND OLD MAN MERRIDEW, WANTED FOR MURDER AND CATTLE THEFT.

LOGAN S. ROOTS
U.S. MARSHAL

# CHAPTER 4

OUTSIDE IN THE street, a drunken cowhand whooped as he raced his horse past the Drover's Cottage. In the dining room, with its tables covered with linen cloths, it was very still.

"It's my duty to take you in."

"I know it is."

"The hell with it!" Ben said. "If you were guilty, I'd take you in, but they'll send you to Texas for trial, with Parkman telling the judge what to do. I'll resign first."

Bijah Catlow leaned back in his chair and glanced around the room. Only a few of the tables were occupied by cattlemen, cattle buyers, or land speculators.

"Ben, you're buying me the best supper this place can offer, with the best wine . . . and they tell me these cattle buyers have fancy tastes. After that," he leaned his forearms on the table, "you're going to arrest me and take me to Fort Smith."

"The devil I will!"

"Look, you're the law. You couldn't be anything else if you tried. If you resign now you've lost all you've gained. You go ahead and take me in. It'll be all right."

Ben Cowan started to protest, but he knew it was just what might be expected from a hotheaded, temperamental, impulsive cowhand like Bijah Catlow.

"What about Rio and the Old Man?"

Catlow gave him a saturnine grin. "Now, Ben, you know me better than that. I picked up that telegram about an hour ago, so naturally I stopped by camp first. After all, I had money for them.

"Somehow or other those boys just naturally saw this here telegram and by this time they're far down the trail to somewhere. You can look for 'em if you want to waste time, but you won't find 'em in a coon's age."

"Bijah, don't be a damned fool. You leave out of here now and I'll give you an hour's start. If I know you, you won't need any more than that. You know Parkman has the courts in his pocket. He'll see you hang."

Catlow picked up the chilled wine bottle and filled their glasses. "That waiter's too durned slow." He looked up, his eyes dancing with deviltry. "Sure, you're right as rain. Parkman will sure enough try to string me up, but remember this, Ben, it's a long way from here to Texas!"

———

TWO WEEKS LATER Ben Cowan looked up from his desk where he was making out his final report.

Roots stopped by the desk. "Your transfer came through, Ben. You go to New Mexico." He turned away, then stopped again. "Oh, by the way, that prisoner you brought in . . . Catlow, was it? He escaped."

*"Escaped?"*

"Uh-huh . . . four or five riders held up the stage and took him off."

"Anybody hurt?"

"Hell, no. From what I hear Catlow had made friends with everybody on the coach, including the driver, and they were glad to see him get away. We did get an identification of one of the men in the bunch that took him, though. The officer escorting Catlow recognized one of the men as Rio Bray."

Bijah Catlow had been right . . . it was a long way to Texas.

———

THE LEGEND OF Bijah Catlow had begun before this, but from this point on, it grew rapidly. The Houston & Texas Central was held up, and Catlow received the credit, whether he was guilty or not. Of one thing men were certain: Bijah Catlow had not forgotten Parkman.

Parkman sent three herds to Kansas the following year, and lost the first one before it was fairly into the Nation. Somebody stampeded the herd, and it vanished.

Nobody could offer more than a guess at what happened to it. Herds of three thousand head are not swallowed by the earth, yet vanish they did.

Meanwhile, it suddenly appeared that Bijah Catlow had registered a brand, the Eight eighty-eight Bar, and around the chuck wagons and in the saloons throughout Texas, men began to chuckle. For three eights and a bar could very neatly swallow Parkman's OP Bar . . . and apparently they had done just that.

Catlow was never at home, but a very tough, very seasoned cowman, Houston Sharkey, was . . . he was not only at home, he was at home with a Winchester and a crew of hard-bitten cowhands who kept strays out of the Eight eighty-eight Bar grazing lands, and allowed no casual visitors.

Several times the law came looking for Catlow, and they were welcomed to look around all they wished.

Parkman came, too, and he came with a couple of tough hands, threatening to butcher a steer and read the hide from the wrong side, where the alteration of the brand would be plain to anyone.

Sharkey levered a shell into the chamber of his Winchester. "You go right ahead, *Colonel* Parkman," he said, "and you better hope that it's an altered brand, because if it isn't I'm going to lay you dead right where the steer lies."

Parkman looked at Houston Sharkey and the Winchester. He looked at the roped steer. He was sure that it was an altered brand . . . *but suppose it wasn't?*

If it was not, he had called this man a thief, an insult anywhere, and no court in the country would convict Sharkey of murder. Not with the viewpoint of Texans what it was at the time.

Parkman looked, hesitated, and backed down. But he went away boiling mad, determined to catch both Catlow and Sharkey.

Two weeks later a tall, cold-eyed rider headed into the rough country south of the Nueces—a tall man with a Winchester and a tied-down gun.

Bijah Catlow spoke Spanish as well as any Mexican in the country. He spoke it smoothly and easily to the señoritas, and he was a popular man about Piedras Negras, across the river from Eagle Pass. He laughed easily, was friendly, and swapped horses and bought drinks. He was so popular that when the tall, cold-eyed man rode into town and asked questions, Catlow was informed within half an hour.

There had been rumors that Parkman had sent a hired killer after him, and the rumors had reached Catlow as well as most of the population of the Mexican village.

Matt Giles was a methodical man. He had begun his killing as a mere boy in the Moderators and Regulators wars of northeast Texas, and had graduated to a sharpshooter in the Confederate Army.

Discharged when the war ended, he drifted back to Texas and the word got around that he was a safe, reliable man for the kind of job he did. Parkman had retained him twice before this.

Matt Giles had never seen Bijah Catlow, but he had listened to all the stories, knew what he looked like, and privately decided that Catlow was a bag of wind. Arrived in Piedras Negras, he had no trouble locating Catlow—he was the talk of the town.

The local law approached Bijah . . . in fact, they had been drinking and poker-playing companions for some weeks now.

"Our jail," the person of the law suggested, "will hold another prisoner . . . for years, if necessary. This man—this Señor Giles—I could arrest him."

"Leave him alone," Bijah said. "If he wants me, I'll make it easy for him."

Bijah Catlow, whose entire life had been predicated on the impulsive and the unregulated, suddenly became the most regulated of men. He took to rising at a certain hour, going to the cantina at a certain hour, taking a siesta according to Mexican custom, and exercising his horse by a ride each afternoon, and each afternoon he went the same way.

The people of Piedras Negras watched and worried. Bijah Catlow was, indeed, making it easy for the gringo killer.

Giles watched, and studied Catlow's movements. Never having known the man, he could not guess his pattern of living had been altered, and to such a methodical man as Giles, the methodical ways of Catlow seemed right and logical.

Carefully, he studied the route to the cantina, but it offered no good cover. By this time Giles knew that Bijah had friends in Piedras Negras, and he knew there might be trouble before he got away. Therefore the killing had to be done where he was offered a good chance of escape, and where he could, preferably, kill with one shot.

Going to or from the cantina, Catlow was always surrounded by a group of friends, and it soon became obvious to Giles that the only place where a killing would be safe would be along the road where Catlow exercised his horse. It also became obvious that along this route there was only one place that offered Giles the opportunity he wanted.

There was a pile of boulders and brush about sixty yards from the trail Catlow rode, and a gully behind that pile which offered a hidden approach to the position. It was made to order.

Giles was a painstaking man, but not an imaginative one, and it was his lack of imagination that brought him to the fatal climax. He watched, and he made his choice, and on the seventh day after his arrival in Piedras Negras he slipped out of town and took his position among the rocks. He sighted the exact spot where Catlow's head would be, planned his second and third shots if such were needed—although they never had been.

Then he settled down among the rocks and waited.

Suddenly, some distance off, he saw Catlow coming, riding easily on the handsome black horse. Giles felt a moment of swift envy . . . *how he would have loved to own that horse!*

He lifted his rifle and waited. Only a few minutes more.

Suddenly the rider on the black horse veered sharply from the trail, and Giles swore. *Now, what the—!*

An instant later a voice behind him said, "Fooled you, didn't we?"

It is given to few men to know the moment of death, but Matt Giles knew it then. With a kind of wild despair he knew he had been trapped, but he was game. He wheeled and fired.

Two bullets tore into him, one going through his shoulder and emerging from the front of his chest, leaving a wound spattered with bone splinters. The second went into his ribs, and for the first and last time he looked directly into the eyes of Bijah Catlow.

His own bullet whistled away into thin, thin air, high above the Mexican landscape.

———

PARKMAN LAY IN his four-poster bed staring up at the ceiling. He had spent a restless night. In fact, he had spent several restless nights since receiving word from Giles in Eagle Pass that he had found Catlow.

Each day he looked forward to the news of the death of Bijah Catlow.

Finally, he could stand it no longer to stay in bed, and he got up and dressed. As he entered the kitchen he stopped abruptly. The table was littered with dirty dishes . . . his best dishes, brought from Carolina.

Nobody, simply nobody used those dishes but himself, and then only when he entertained guests more distinguished than the usual run.

Also, the cook was not at work, and he should have been up—Parkman glanced at his watch—at least an hour ago.

Parkman was a man who came easily to anger, and he was angry now. He stepped out the door toward the bunkhouse and was brought up short.

Something was wrong—radically wrong.

The corral was empty of horses. The bunkhouse was dark and silent, and over each bunkhouse window was a blanket, hung on the outside of the building. From the doorknob to a snubbing post ran a rope, holding the door shut, and against the snubbing post was tied a double-barreled shotgun aimed at the bunkhouse door. It was rigged in such a way that anybody tugging on the doorknob from the inside would fire both barrels of the shotgun. It was obvious that nobody had tried, so those within must have been informed of this.

Parkman went to the post and gingerly unlimbered the shotgun. Then opened the door to the bunkhouse.

"What the hell's going on around here?" he shouted. "By the Lord Harry, I've had enough of these practical jokes, and—"

From the corner of his eye he caught a glimpse of

his front porch, invisible to him until now. There, seated in his own favorite chair on the broad veranda was somebody. . . . Parkman shouted, but there was no reply.

Finally given somebody on whom he could vent his anger, Parkman started for the front porch, almost running. The stranger sat with his hat over his eyes, apparently asleep.

Leaping up on the porch, Parkman jerked the hat away, his mouth opened to roar angry words.

And he looked into the still, cold eyes of Matt Giles.

By nightfall the story was told in every bunkhouse within miles, and within a few days it was riding north with the trail herds.

Parkman had sent a paid killer after Bijah Catlow, and his killer had been returned . . . dead.

Moreover, Bijah had stolen Parkman's corral of fine riding stock, including his own favorite mounts. He had eaten in Parkman's own house, and on his best dishes. Even Parkman's own riders chuckled.

When they buried Matt Giles they noted the position of the wounds, and speculated. Catlow had outsmarted the hired gunman, had come up behind him, given him his chance, and it was quite obvious that Giles had been shot as he turned.

From Piedras Negras the rest of the story was not slow to arrive.

And the legend of Bijah Catlow added another chapter.

# CHAPTER 5

D EPUTY UNITED STATES Marshal Ben Cowan rode into New Mexico to conduct a quiet investigation into the reported theft of cattle by Comanches, cattle which were traded to Comancheros and sold in New Mexico or elsewhere. Several Texans had created incidents by riding into New Mexico to recover stolen cattle. Childress had done so, as had Hittson, and they had driven the recovered cattle back to Texas. There had been some shooting, and there was apt to be more.

Cowan heard of the killing of Matt Giles by Catlow before he ever left Fort Smith. He was not surprised. That Parkman had been behind Matt Giles's mission was obvious, although it was impossible to prove. Giles had been the wrong man to send after Catlow. He was too methodical. A man of method himself, Cowan knew that against Catlow method was not enough. Bijah was a man of quick, instinctive imagination, and might on impulse discard all the accepted ways of doing things and do something radically different.

Whatever their former relationship, Cowan and Catlow were now unalterably opposed. There was a line beyond which a man might not go, even in the tolerant West. Cowan had himself been a cowhand, and knew enough of conditions in Texas to feel Catlow and his friends were right in branding and driving to sale their herd of mavericks. The killing of Giles was obviously self-defense, but when Catlow drove off Parkman's saddle stock he had stepped beyond the pale.

Many were amused, but all recognized it had been a theft. In Laredo, Catlow shot an officer who attempted to arrest him and escaped below the border. It was apparent that Catlow had accepted the role of the outlaw.

As for the train robbery, Ben Cowan was sure that had been done by the Sam Bass gang, but Catlow got the credit—at least in the minds of some.

For three months Ben Cowan rode the lonely trails of New Mexico. He trailed outlaws, dodged Apaches, accepted meals at lonely sheep camps or ranches, and drifted on.

He said he was hunting range and planning to settle, that he was intending to trail a herd from Texas, but would buy cattle in New Mexico to avoid the drive, if the price was right.

This was a feeler—a lead to the Comancheros who might have stolen Texas cattle to sell. He was too wise to push that aspect, and devoted most of his time to scouting range. This he could do in all seriousness, for he really intended to find a ranch for himself.

He scouted along the Pecos and the Rio Grande, talked to ranchers and soldiers, but made no inquiries about cattle. Here and there he did mention returning to Texas to buy cattle, and he talked with those who had made the drive to ask about water holes and grazing.

They were long, grueling rides in the sun and the

wind, but from them Ben Cowan rapidly picked up some knowledge of the New Mexico country, located two stolen herds, and reported to the main office.

A reserved and self-contained man, Ben Cowan was warm-hearted and pleasant by nature, but he was also a hunter. A hunter—not a killer. Yet if need be he could kill, as he had demonstrated against the Tonkawa outlaws and others. Still, by instinct he was a hunter, a man who understood trailing, but even more, a man who understood the mind of the pursued.

A lonely man, he had always envied Bijah his easy friendliness, the casual grace with which he made strangers into friends, and seemed never to offend anyone.

Once, when only a boy, he had heard a man say to his father: "Yes, it is a beautiful country, but it must be made safe for honest people, for women and children. It must become a country to live in, not just a country to loot and leave. Too many," the man had said, "come merely to get rich and get out. I want to stay. For that we need law, we need justice, and we need a place where homes can be built. *Homes,* I say, not just houses."

Somehow from that day on Ben was dedicated. He, too, wanted to see homes. He wanted friends to talk with in the evening, children for his children to play with. And for that there must be peace.

Beyond a daily paper when one was available, he had read little. He was a grave, thoughtful man, but a keen sense of humor was hidden behind his quiet face. No doubt there were those who thought him dull. But he missed nothing, and at heart he was a sympathetic man, understanding even of the outlaws he pursued.

He was happiest on a trail, and the more difficult the trail, the happier he became. He knew wild country, knew it in all the subtle changes of light and shadow, knew the ways of birds and the habits of men and animals. So much was common sense. Men who travel need water, fuel, grass for their horses, and food for themselves. All of these are restricting factors, limiting the areas of escape.

Given a general knowledge of the country, a grasp of a man's nature, and his needs, a trail could often be followed without even seeing anything upon the ground. And a man who knows wild country is never actually a stranger to any wild land.

Landforms fall into patterns, as do the actions of men. The valley, hill, and ridge, the occurrence of springs and the flow of water—these follow patterns of their own. Many a guide or scout in Indian country had never seen the country over which they scouted—but they had lived in the wilds.

Men who live always in cities rarely notice the sky . . . they do not know the stars or the cloud forms, they are skeptical of what a man can read in what is to themselves only a blank page. To Ben Cowan every yard of country he crossed could be read like a page of print. He knew what animals and insects were there, what each tiny trail in the sand might mean. He knew that certain birds never fly a great distance from water; that certain insects need water for their daily existence; and that some birds or animals can go days without any water at all except what they get from the plant growth about them.

So Ben Cowan rode the lonely hills with a mind alive and alert, noticing everything, adding this thing to that . . . always aware.

Tucson was baking in a hot July sun when he rode into town. There was little enough to see, but to a man who had not slept in a bed for more than a month and had not seen more than three buildings in a bunch in four times that long, it looked pretty good.

Ben Cowan studied the town thoughtfully from under the brim of his white hat.

Flat-roofed adobes and *jacals* made of mesquite poles and the long wands of the ocotillo plastered with adobe made up more than two-thirds of the town. Main Street was lined with pack trains just in from Sonora, and a long bull train was unloading freight on a side street.

Ben left his roan at a livery stable and walked up the street to the Shoo-Fly Restaurant. It was a long, low-ceilinged room, rather narrow, with a scattering of tables covered with table cloths, red and white checkered. He dropped into a chair with a sigh and looked at the menu.

### BREAKFAST
*Fried venison and chili*
*Bread and coffee with milk*

### DINNER
*Roast venison and chili*
*Chili frijoles*
*Chili on tortillas*
*Tea and coffee with milk*

SUPPER
*Chili, from 4 o'clock on*

Ben glanced hastily at the clock on the shelf: 3:45.

"Roast venison," he said, "and quick, before the time runs out."

The Mexican girl flashed him a quick smile. "I see," she said.

A moment later she was back. "No more," she said regretfully. "All gone."

"You tell Mrs. Wallen"—the voice that spoke behind him was familiar—"that I said this man was a friend of mine—or was last time I saw him."

Bijah Catlow . . .

Ben looked up. "Sit down, Bijah." And then as Bijah dropped into his seat, Ben added, "You're under arrest."

Bijah chuckled. "The .45 I've got trained on your belly under the table says I'm not. Anyway, you'd better eat up. I never like to shoot a man who's hungry."

A slim brown arm came over Ben's shoulder with a plate of roast venison and chili, frijoles, tortillas. In the other hand was a pot of coffee.

# CHAPTER 6

BIJAH CATLOW LEANED his forearms on the table, and shoved his hat on the back of his head. He grinned widely at Ben.

"Eat up, *amigo*, and listen to your Uncle Dudley. You're wastin' your time. You throw that badge out the window and come in with me . . . you'll make more in a couple of weeks than you'll make on that job in twenty years."

"Can't do it, Bijah. And the word is out on you. You're to be picked up where and when."

"Look." Bijah leaned closer. "I need you. I need a man I can count on, Ben. This here thing I've got lined up is the biggest . . . well, nothin' was ever any bigger. One job an' we've got it made . . . all of us. But I need you, Ben."

"Sorry."

"Don't be a damn' fool, boy. I know what you make on that job, an' I know you. You like the good things as much as I do. You come along with me, an' after that you can go straight.

"Hell, Ben, after this one I'm goin' to take my end of it an' light out. Goin' to Oregon or somewheres like that an' get myself a place." He flushed suddenly, and looked embarrassed, for the first time that Ben could remember. "Maybe I'll get married."

"Got somebody in mind?"

Bijah looked at him quickly. "Why not? Look, Ben, I'm not the crazy damn' fool you figure me for. I want to marry and have some kids my own self. That Parkman . . . if it hadn't been for him I'd probably never have got myself mixed up."

"You stole his horses."

Bijah shot him a quick look. "Yeah . . . that did it, didn't it?"

"And there was that officer."

"He would've killed me, Ben. He was figurin' to take me in, dead meat. It was him or me."

"Maybe . . . but you were on the wrong side of the law. Odd, you gents never seem to realize that when you cross the law you set yourself up for anybody's gun. And you can't win, Bijah. You just can't."

Ben gulped the scalding black coffee and then he said, "Bijah, give yourself up. Surrender right now, to me. I'll take you in, and I'll do everything I can to see that you get a fair shake. If you don't, I've got to come after you."

Bijah stared gloomily out the window. "There's this girl, Ben. I don't figure she'd wait . . . or maybe there ain't enough between us to make her want to wait." Suddenly, he grinned. "Damn it, Ben, you nearly had me talked into it. I was forgettin' what I've got lined up." He called for coffee, and then he said, "Ben, how about it?"

"What?"

"You ride with me on this job?" He leaned closer. "Hell, Ben, it ain't even in this country!"

"I wouldn't break anybody's law, Bijah. You know that. Their law's as good as ours. If I respect my own laws, I have to respect theirs."

"Aw, you're crazy!" Bijah stared ruefully into his coffee. "I never figured you would, but damn it, Ben, I wish we was on the same side!"

"I wish we were, too."

Bijah looked up, his eyes dancing with deviltry. "Somebody will have to kill you, Ben. I'm afraid I will."

"I hope you never try. You're a good man, Bijah, but I'll beat you."

"You hardheaded, hard-nosed ol' wolf!" Bijah said. He was suddenly cheerful. "Did you come here after me?"

"How could I? Nobody knew where you were. I'm sorry you're here. Now I'll have to arrest you."

Bijah chuckled. "That head of yours never could see more than one trail at a time. Damn you, Ben, I want you to meet my girl. She lives here in Tucson."

"I'd like to meet her."

Bijah wiped his mouth with the back of his hand and dug out the makings. "She don't know about me, Ben. She thinks I'm a rancher." He looked up quickly. "Well, after this deal I will be!"

Ben was suddenly tired. He ate mechanically while Bijah sat across the table from him. Bijah was the last man he had wanted to see, yet if there was any way, any at all, he meant to take him in. Oddly enough, he knew Catlow expected it of him, and respected him for it.

Nor was there any sense in trying to persuade Catlow. He had tried that, knowing before he began that he was wasting his time. The big Irishman was a stubborn man. Ben looked across the table at him, suddenly realizing he had always known that someday it would come to a showdown between them. They had always respected each other, but had always been on opposite sides of the fence.

What was Catlow planning? It was out of the country, he had said, and that could scarcely mean anywhere but Mexico. And there was already enough strain between the two countries. But Catlow always got along well with the Mexicans—he liked them and they liked him.

Whatever it was Catlow planned, Ben Cowan must stop him. And the simplest way was to get him into jail.

"You said you had a gun under the table. I don't believe it."

Catlow grinned. "Don't make me prove it. It was in the top of my boot, and now it's in my lap. Minute ago I had it up my sleeve, but always in my mitt. Yeah," he added, "I'd never take a chance on you. You're too damn' good with a gun."

"All right, I'll take your word for it, Bijah. But you hand over the gun and I'll take you in—do it now before you go so far there's no turning back."

Catlow was suddenly serious again. "Not a chance, Ben. This deal I've got lined up—I'll never have a chance like this again, and neither will you. The hell of it is . . . Ben, there isn't a man in that outfit I can count on when the chips are down.

"Oh, there's a couple of them will stick. The Old Man, now. He's one to ride the river with, but he hasn't got the savvy I need. I need somebody who can adjust to a quick change, somebody who can take over if I'm not Johnny-on-the-spot. And you're it."

The Mexican girl refilled their cups and Ben

glanced around the room. It was almost empty, and nobody was within earshot—not the way they had been talking.

Gloomily, he reflected there was no way to stop Bijah from going ahead with this deal, whatever it was. Only jail.

And Bijah was too filled with savvy to be tricked into jail.

Nor was it time for a gun battle. That was the last thing he wanted. In the first place, he liked Bijah, and had no desire to shoot him; and in the second place . . . It was like Hickok and Hardin . . . neither wanted a fight, because even if one beat the other he'd probably die in the process. Ben was sure that he was faster and a better shot than Bijah, though with mighty little margin. That would matter, but not much, because Bijah Catlow was game. You might get lead into him, but he'd kill you for it. He would go down shooting.

Ben Cowan knew too much about guns to believe that old argument that a .45 always knocked a man down. Whoever said that knew very little about guns. If a man was killing mad and coming at you, a .45 wouldn't stop him. You had to hit him right through the heart, the brain, or on a large bone to stop him . . . and there had been cases where even that wouldn't do the job. He knew of dozens of cases where it had not stopped a man, and Bijah Catlow would not stop for it.

Ben recalled a case where two men walked toward each other shooting—starting only thirty feet apart—and each scored four hits out of six shots while getting hit with .45-calibre slugs.

Bijah leaned over the table again. "Look, Ben, while you're in Tucson, why not declare a truce? Then you make your try any time I'm out of town."

"Sorry."

Bijah got up. "Have it your own way, then." The derringer he held in his big hand was masked from the rest of the room by the size of his hand. "You just sit tight."

He stepped to the door, then disappeared through it, but Ben Cowan made no move to follow. The time was not now.

It would come.

———

MEN WHO ARE much alone, when meeting with other people either talk too much or become taciturn. Ben Cowan was of the latter sort. He had a genuine liking for people, finding qualities to appreciate in even the worst of them, but usually he was silent, an onlooker rather than a participant.

People who saw Catlow for the first time knew him immediately for a tough, dangerous man. But with Ben, although people might take a second look at him, it was only the old-timers who sized him up as a man to leave alone. It is a fact that really dangerous men often do not look it.

Strolling to the edge of the boardwalk, Ben looked down the busy street, letting all his senses take in the town. His eyes, his ears, his nose were alert, and something else . . . that subtle intuitive sense that allows certain men to perceive undercurrents, movements, and changes in atmosphere.

Bijah Catlow had disappeared, but the Mexican

half a block away who was too obviously ignoring Ben Cowan would probably be Catlow's man.

Ben Cowan took a cigar from his pocket and lighted it. He was in no hurry, being a man of deliberation, and he knew that taking Catlow would be quite a trick. And Bijah had obviously made friends in Tucson. Moreover, a substantial portion of the population were something less than law-abiding; and as for the rest, they believed every man should saddle his own broncs. If Cowan wanted Catlow, let him take him.

Vigilante activity in California, and Ranger activity in Texas had contributed to the population of the Territory, but the population had always been a rugged lot, who fought Apaches as a matter of course.

The town was an old one—not so old as Santa Fe, of course, but it had been founded shortly after 1768 on the site of an Indian village, or in its close vicinity. There were Spanish-speaking settlers on the spot as well as Indians when Anza passed by on his way to California.

Ben Cowan had no plans. Catlow had mentioned a girl, but Ben shied from that aspect. Bijah had said he wanted him to meet her, and he was undoubtedly sincere, but Ben was uneasy around women, and he had known few except casual acquaintances around dance halls.

His mother had died in childbirth and he had grown up on a ranch among men, nursed first by a Mexican woman, and after she left, he was free to wander about as he pleased. Moreover, he was going to put the cuffs on Bijah, and he wanted no weepy woman involved.

Actually, he had little time to consider Bijah, for the man he had really come for was somewhere in the area. Ben had trailed him down the Salt River Canyon, through Apache country, and then had lost him somewhere to the north but headed in this direction.

Word had reached him at Fort Apache that a deserter named Miller had ambushed the Army paymaster and escaped with more than nine thousand dollars. He had been heard to refer, sometime before, to a brother in Tucson.

Ben Cowan had picked up the trail and followed his man into the town, where Miller had promptly dropped from sight.

Miller first, Cowan decided, and then Catlow.

Ben turned and strolled on down the street. Evening was coming on and the wagons were beginning to disappear from the street. A few men had already started to drift toward that part of town known as the Barrio Libre—the Free Quarter. Ben glanced that way, and then after a few minutes of thought, turned toward the Quartz Rock Saloon.

The bartender looked up as he entered, noticing the badge but offering no comment.

"Make it a beer," Ben said, and then added, "A friend of mine in Silver City said I should drop in here."

The bartender drew the beer and placed it on the bar before Cowan.

"His name was Sandoval," Ben said.

The bartender picked up the beer and wiped under it with his bar cloth. "What do you want to know?"

"The name is Miller. He may have other names.

He rode into town within the last forty-eight hours. He may have a brother here."

The bartender put the mug down. "Are you lookin' for anybody else?"

Ben Cowan did not hesitate. "Not looking. I want Miller."

"It ain't a brother . . . it's a brother-in-law, and he's no friend of Miller's—only there ain't much he can do about it. Miller is a bad one." The bartender leaned his thick forearms on the bar. "Only he'd better walk a straight line this time. Bijah Catlow is courtin' Cord Burton."

"Cord?"

"Short for Cordelia, daughter to Moss Burton, Miller's brother-in-law. From what I hear tell, Catlow is an impatient man."

Ben Cowan took a swallow of his beer. So there was to be no waiting . . . everything seemed to point him toward Bijah Catlow.

He finished his beer and left the change from five dollars lying on the bar. As he turned away he was remembering what he knew about Miller.

The man had ambushed that paymaster. Moreover, every indication offered by his trail west implied that he was a sly, careful man. If such a man thought Catlow was a danger to him he would not say so to his face. He would wait, watch, and if possible kill him.

Bijah was a tough man but a reckless one. Did he know how dangerous Miller could be?

# CHAPTER 7

BEN COWAN HAD an uncomfortable feeling that events were building toward a climax that had no place in his planning.

It was true that he wanted to arrest Bijah Catlow and get him out of the way before he got into more trouble. It was also true that it was his duty to arrest him, as Bijah himself well knew. Yet first things came first, and in Ben's plans Miller was first in line. But now the trail to Miller led him right to Catlow.

He made no more inquiries, nor did he manifest any interest in Miller. Tucson was not a large town, and it was easy to find out what he needed to know by listening or by dropping a discreet comment.

He learned that Moss Burton was well thought of locally. He owned a saddle shop, and had some small interest in mining properties, as did almost everyone else in town. Besides his daughter Cordelia, he had two small sons; his wife had taught for a while in the first school organized by the Anglo-Saxon element.

In discussing Burton, it was natural that Miller's name would come up. Miller was a tough man, and Moss Burton was no fighter, so Miller had promptly moved in. Also, he was married to Mrs. Burton's sister.

By the time two days had passed Ben Cowan knew where Miller kept his horse, knew who his friends

were, and which places in the Barrio Libre he preferred to others. He also knew that Miller was involved with a young Mexican woman, a widow, and
trouble was expected, for her brothers disapproved.

Ben was quite sure that Miller did not know he
had been followed to Tucson. Apparently he had
been cautious just because it was his way . . . but Ben
Cowan took nothing for granted. He wanted Miller,
but he wanted him alive if possible.

Twice he saw Miller on the street, but each time he
was close to women or children, and in no place to
start anything, and Ben Cowan was not an impatient
man. On his third day in town, Ben Cowan saw the
Mexican.

He came up the street riding a hammer-headed
roan horse that had been doing some running. He
carried a carbine in his hand, wore two belt guns, one
butt forward, one back, and crossed cartridge belts
on his chest. His wide-bottomed buckskin pants had
been slit to reveal fancy cowhide boots, and spurs
with rowels bigger than pesos. The Mexican had a
scar down one cheek and a thick mustache.

The Mexican rode to the Quartz Rock Saloon and
dismounted there. He kept his carbine in his hand
when he went inside. A few moments later, Ben saw a
Mexican boy leave the back of the saloon. Ben drew
back into the doorway of a vacant adobe and lighted
a fresh cigar. Soon the Mexican boy returned.

Ben studied the roan. The brand was unfamiliar,
and looked like a Mexican brand. The horse had
come a long way, by the look of him, as had the man.
But that was a rugged character, that Mexican sol-

dier, and the ride would not show on him as it would on the horse . . . or on several horses.

Soldier? Now, why had he thought *that?* He could put his finger on no reason, yet he must have sensed something about the man—call it a hunch. And Ben was not a man who fought his hunches. Too often they had proved out.

A Mexican soldier here probably meant a deserter— and from just where?

A horse came up the street at a fast walk and Ben drew deeper into the shadows. The rider was Catlow, who dismounted and went inside.

Catlow had come from the direction the boy had taken. It did not follow there had to be a connection, but it seemed likely.

It was strictly by chance that Ben heard the voices.

The doorway in which he stood was set back from the walk by at least two paces. The window of the adjoining building—the side window—was only a couple of paces farther back. What he heard was a girl's voice.

"Kinfolk he may be, but he's none of our blood, Pa, and if you don't tell him to go, I shall."

"Now, now, Cordelia, you can't do that! You can't just throw a man out of the house for nothing."

"He's a thief, Pa, and probably worse. You know it, and I do."

There was silence within, and Ben Cowan waited. He did not like to eavesdrop on private conversations, but in this case it was his business to do so, for without doubt they were talking of Miller.

"Pa, he's afraid of somebody . . . or something. He

never steps into the street without looking out the window first."

Her father was silent for several minutes, and then he said, "I know it, Cordelia." A pause. "Cordelia, I can order him from our home, but what if he refuses to go? I was not in the war . . . I've never used a gun but once or twice. I doubt," he added, "whether any other man in Tucson can say that, and living in the country as we do, I am surprised that I can."

"I would not want you to fight him."

"If he refuses to go, what else could I do? I am afraid, Cordelia, that women sometimes make demands on their men without realizing the consequences."

Ben Cowan had lost interest, for the time being, in Bijah Catlow and the Mexican soldier. For a moment he considered going in the shop next door and asking them to invite him to supper . . . then he could leave with Miller and make his arrest. But to do such a thing might endanger the Burtons, and he had no right to bring trouble to innocent people.

Miller was a cross-grained man with a hard, arrogant way about him, a man born to cause trouble wherever he might go. Ben Cowan tried to imagine Miller in the same house with Catlow, and could not; for Miller's attitude was just that calculated to move Bijah to action.

A door closed and Ben Cowan stiffened, glancing swiftly to right and left . . . could it have been the shop door? He heard no voices—only the pound of a hammer on leather. He started to step from the doorway and found himself face to face with Cordelia Burton. He swept off his hat.

"I beg your pardon," he said, greatly embarrassed. "I—"

She glanced from him to the window, then abruptly walked on. He was about to speak, but held his tongue. He remained there, staring after her. She was lovely, undeniably lovely . . . she was also very definitely a girl who knew her own mind. After a moment of consideration, Ben decided that she was not overmatched in coping with Bijah, for Bijah was basically a gentleman. Miller was another item, another item entirely.

Annoyed with himself, Ben started for the Quartz Rock. He felt a fool, being caught eavesdropping by such a girl, and he had stared at her like a damned fool.

Cordelia Burton walked on down the boardwalk, her heels clicking. The momentary irritation she had felt on seeing the man standing where he could obviously hear all that was said within passed away, but she was puzzled.

The man was a stranger . . . a tall man with broad shoulders. In the shadow of the building she had seen only his chin, but he had spoken courteously and she had been wrong not to acknowledge it. Who could he be? And why would he be standing there?

The building was empty. There was nothing nearby, unless . . . unless for some reason he was watching for somebody at the Quartz Rock. Suddenly she had a distinct impression that there had been a badge on his chest.

Badges were not frequent in Tucson, and she had never seen a man who resembled this one wearing a badge. He had been standing in the dark doorway of an abandoned building watching somebody or something. She flushed as she realized how self-centered she must have been to be so sure he had been listening in on her conversation. She paused on the corner.

She knew she had best be getting home. It was late, and a decent woman kept off the streets at this hour. Yet her curiosity made her turn to look back. The man she had seen was crossing the street toward the Quartz Rock Saloon. At the same time she noticed Bijah Catlow's horse tied to the rail.

She would ask Bijah—he would certainly know something about the tall stranger with the badge.

Suddenly, from behind her she heard the quick step of a fast-walking horse, and it loomed darkly beside her. Despite herself, she looked up, and when she did so she recognized the chin.

"Beggin' your pardon, ma'am, it's late for a lady to be out. If you'll permit, I'll just ride along to see you get home safe."

"Thank you."

Oddly enough, she felt shaky inside—an unusual sort of trembling feeling. But she kept on walking, looking straight ahead. After a moment, he spoke again.

"Ma'am, I couldn't help overhearing back there." So he *had* been listening! Her lips tightened. "If you'll allow me to say so, you shouldn't urge your pa to kick Miller out. He might try it."

"And so?"

"You know the answer to that. Miller might kill him. More probably he'd shame him, which would be worse. It's a bad thing for a man to be shamed in front of his womenfolks . . . it's sometimes worse than bein' killed. If he was shamed, he might get a gun and try it on Miller."

Cordelia was appalled. Suddenly, for the first time, she realized what her indignation might mean to her father. Of course, Miller would not go unless he wanted to, and the thought of her father trying to face Miller with a gun touched her with icy fear.

"I—I didn't think of that."

"No, ma'am, and you didn't think about stayin' out this late. Supposing some drunk had come up to you and spoke improper. I'd have to speak to him, and he might resent it. First thing, ma'am, there'd be a man killed—and you'd be to blame."

"It was my only chance to speak to Pa alone."

She had reached the gate at her house, and she turned toward him. "Who are you? What are you?"

"Ben Cowan . . . Deputy United States Marshal in the Territory."

"You—you came here after somebody?"

"Miller's my man."

Miller? Then why didn't he arrest him? It would solve everything. She started to say as much, but he spoke first.

"I'll thank you to say nothing to anyone, ma'am. I want to do this in my own good time, and where no-body will be hurt—not even him, if I can help it." He turned his horse. "Evening, ma'am."

He rode away up the street, gone before she could thank him. She went through the gate, closing it behind her, then paused in the darkness to look after him. He was briefly seen against the window lights of a saloon.

Bijah Catlow was sitting at the table talking to her

mother as she placed the silver. He looked around at Cordelia. "I near came after you," he said. "It's no time for a decent girl to be out."

"That's what Marshal Cowan said."

Bijah gave a start. "Ben Cowan? You met him?"

When she explained he asked, too quickly, "Did he tell you anything about me?"

"No." She was surprised. "I had no idea you even knew each other."

"Since we were boys. He's a good man, Ben is. One of the best." He looked at her again. "Cord, did he say why he was here?"

She hesitated a moment. "No," she said.

Pa would be coming along soon, and Miller, too. Miller had not met Catlow yet.

Suddenly the door opened and Miller came in—a lean, rangy man with hollow cheeks and sour, suspicious eyes. He shot a quick look at Catlow, and Cordelia introduced them.

Catlow's forearms lay upon the table. He looked up from under his shaggy brows, cataloguing Miller at a glance. "Howdy," he said carelessly.

"Mr. Miller is married to my mother's sister." Cordelia decided she would make it plain at once that there was no blood relationship. "He is visiting us for a few days."

Miller gave her a hard look at the words, "a few days." Then he said, "I got to be around longer'n I figured."

There was a step on the porch outside and Bijah noted the quick way in which Miller turned to face the door. Moss Burton came in.

"I'm driftin' south," Catlow said. He had sensed

the situation quickly, recalling words he had heard dropped before this. "Why don't you ride along with me?" He put his eyes hard on Miller. "Men like you or me, we sleep better outside, anyway."

The stillness that entered the room made Cordelia hold her breath. She hesitated, ever so slightly, before placing the last plate upon the table.

"When I'm ready," Miller said, "I'll go."

Catlow looked up at him and cold amusement flickered in his eyes.

"Get ready," he said.

# CHAPTER 8

THOUGH MILLER WAS a cautious man, now fury burst like a bomb in the pit of his stomach. He kept his eyes on his plate, but it was only with an effort that he fought back the urge to lunge across the table at Catlow. He forced himself to take a bite of food and to begin chewing.

"This is your doin'," he said to Cordelia. "I don't like it."

"When you come visiting again," she replied coolly, "we will be glad to see you . . . if you bring Aunt Ellie." Then with an edge to her voice she asked, "By the way, where is Aunt Ellie?"

"She's in Kansas."

"We'd love to see her. She is always welcome here."

Moss Burton had started in from the kitchen, where he had gone to wash his hands. Now, desperately, he wished he had remained there.

Miller saw him and started to accuse him, but Bijah Catlow was nothing if not considerate of the feelings of others. To save Moss the embarrassment of reiterating the request to leave, with all that might follow, Bijah interrupted Miller.

"You ain't goin' to like it around here nohow," he said, grinning cheerfully. "Cordie's got herself a new gentleman friend."

"What's that to me?"

Catlow chuckled, a taunt in his eyes and in his tone. "Figured it might be. It ain't every day a girl has a U.S. Deputy Marshal comin' to set with her."

The hot fury in Miller's belly was gone. Where it had been there was now a cold lump of fear. "I don't believe you," he muttered, and his fingers fumbled with the handle of his coffee cup.

Catlow, who knew what the grapevine was saying, had a sudden hunch and played it. "Army paymaster killed over near Stein's Pass by a deserter. Were you ever in the Army, Miller?"

Miller gulped his coffee to cover his fear. He had seen too much of what United States marshals could do when he had been around Fort Smith. Why had he been such a fool as to ride into Tucson? Too many people knew he had a brother-in-law here.

He would have to get out. To go . . . where? Prescott was out of the question—too many knew him there. Yuma, then? But someone at the Fort might recognize him. The Army was always moving men around . . . and the thought of the Federal pen made him nervous.

"That marshal means nothin' to me, but it's plain enough that I ain't wanted . . . among my own kin." He pushed back his chair and got to his feet, glancing at Bijah, who watched him, amused but alert. "You, I'll see again."

"Right outside the door, if you like," Catlow replied carelessly, "or in front of the Quartz Rock in half an hour."

"I'll pick the time," Miller said, "and the place."

"You an' Matt Giles," Catlow said.

When Miller had gone, Cordelia asked, "What was that about Matt Giles?"

"Man I used to know. Figured Miller might know of him."

Bijah took Cordelia's guitar from its place in the corner and, tuning up, sang "Buffalo Gals," and followed it with "Sweet Betsy from Pike." He sang easily and cheerfully, just as he had sung around many campfires and in bunkhouses. He was a man who did everything well, and he did most things with something of a flair. As he sang, he watched Cordelia.

She was, he thought, a thoroughbred. She had courage, and a cool, quiet strength, but above all she was a lady. Poised, without pretensions, and gracious, she was friendly, yet reserved. What she thought of him, Catlow had no idea. He had met her, asked to call, and had visited the house several times.

Now he was going away, and for the first time he found, with some surprise, that he did not wish to go. He recalled what he had told Cowan about wanting to marry this girl, and he realized he had meant every word of it. Of his life she knew nothing. She assumed he was a cattleman looking for range—a few of them had drifted into Arizona, looking around. Henry C. Hooker had a herd of cattle stampede while driving them through the state for sale to the Army, and when the stampede was over the cattle were grazing around a *ciénaga* in the Sulphur Springs Valley, and it was there he established the Sierra Bonita Ranch. Hooker started it; others had followed. All this was known to every child in the street, and Catlow was so obviously a cattleman.

Cordelia would not have been likely to hear any of

the stories about him, Bijah decided, nor would her father, for that matter. Moss Burton worked over his saddles, boots, and bridles, paying little attention to gossip; he ate his meals at home, and did not frequent the saloons.

As Bijah played, idly strumming the guitar, his thoughts turned to the venture that lay ahead. There were twelve men in his outfit, and several of them were strangers, but they had been selected with as much care as possible. Bijah knew very well what lay before him. He possessed a sharp, intelligent brain, and he was using it in this.

Every detail had been planned. Not only the move south and the taking of the money, but the escape. This, he felt sure, would be the crux of the whole thing. With any kind of luck, they could reach their destination unseen and, if all went well, take the gold. Their great danger lay in their escape, and to this he had given most of his thinking.

If they were captured during their attempt on the gold they would probably be shot; otherwise they would rot in a Mexican jail. The courts were slow, and nobody would be in a hurry to try a bunch of gringos who had come into Mexico looking for trouble.

His band of men had one thing in common: all spoke Spanish, Mexican-style, and all could pass as Mexicans. This would help during the ride south if they were seen, which Catlow hoped would not happen.

One member of his outfit was a half-breed Tarahumara Indian who knew all the secret water holes and rock tanks, places known only to wild animals and wilder Indians. Catlow and his men would avoid the main trails, avoid the Apaches as well, and reach the heart of Sonora unseen.

Not one of the men he had selected was known for having a loose tongue; nevertheless he had told them only a part of his plan. The escape route he kept to himself, and only the two involved knew about his cattle deal.

Impulsive he might be, but Abijah Catlow had done the most careful planning for this big strike. He was going to make this one and get out . . . and then to Oregon and the cattle business.

It was after ten o'clock when he left the Burton house, and he took the precaution of having Cordelia take the lamp into the kitchen before he left by the front door.

When he reached the house where he was living, Old Man Merridew was loafing at the door. "Marshal's inside . . . wants to talk."

Ben Cowan was sitting in the rocker in the dark, and Bijah removed the chimney from the lamp and touched a match to the wick. He replaced the chimney and looked across the lamp, the light throwing highlights and shadows on his strongly boned face.

"You goin' to pull me in?"

"No," Ben replied. "I just came with a friendly word of advice."

Bijah chuckled. "What else did I ever get from you, Ben? What is it now?"

"Miller . . . you've made an enemy there, and the man's dangerous."

"Him? Small potatoes. I ain't beggin' trouble, but if he wants it he can have it."

"Don't low-rate him. He's worse than Giles."

"*Him?*" Catlow repeated skeptically. "Miller? You're loco."

"I know him. I followed him here from New Mexico. The man's a wolf. He'll wait a year, two years if necessary. He's a hater, Bijah. You and me were never that, and a hater is a tough man to best."

"That all you came for?"

"It's a plenty. Did you ever know me to shy from shadows? I know the man."

Catlow sat down and rolled a smoke. "All right. If you say he's that bad, I'll put my money on it."

"I'm going to take him in, but I want him where nobody will get hurt if there's shooting. I can wait, too."

Bijah sat down on the bed and pulled off first one boot and then the other. He sat there, holding the boot in his hand, wriggling his toes into comfort. Then he dropped the boot and removed his gun-belt, tossing it over the post at the head of the bed where it would hang near his hand as he slept.

The coal-oil lamp threw shadows into the corners and behind the old wardrobe. There was little enough in the room. The bed, a straight-backed chair, and the rocker where Ben sat, the wardrobe, a table, bowl and water pitcher. In the corner near the door was Bijah's saddle and his rifle, saddlebags and a blanket-roll.

Ben took a cigar from his pocket and lit up. His eyes dropped to the gear on the floor. There was a canteen there, too. It had been freshly filled. As Bijah had been out, it must have been filled by one of the others—Merridew probably. They were pulling out, then.

"Like to talk you out of this deal you've got," Ben suggested. "You're asking for it."

"Hell!" Catlow said. "I figured you'd be glad to get me out of town—you walkin' my girl home like you done. You tryin' to cut me out?"

Ben Cowan shook his head. "You know better than that. She was on the street alone . . . besides, she caught me listening to talk between her and her father. It was about this Miller . . . she was fixing to get her pa killed."

He got to his feet. "Bijah . . . this is government business if you cross the line into Mexico. It's up to me to stop you."

Bijah grinned at him, peeling off his shirt. He was a well-muscled man, and the muscle was all power, as Ben Cowan had reason to know. "Stop me, then. But I'd still like to have you in with me. You'd be worth the lot of this crowd."

"You'd have to go far to beat the Old Man," Ben said. "That one's an old wolf from the high country. You turn him loose on Miller and you'd have nothing to worry about."

"I fight my own battles."

Ben put on his hat. "Sorry I can't talk you out of this, Bijah, but I didn't much figure I could." He put out his hand. "We'll meet again."

"You keep your ears pinned back when we do, or I'll notch 'em for you. This is the big one for me, Ben, an' all bets are off."

Ben Cowan stepped out into the night and walked

past Merridew, who sat in the darkness near the gate. He went by, and then he came back.

"You know Miller?"

"I know him."

"He's out to get Bijah—sooner or later he'll try."

"Catlow don't need no help."

"I know that. I carry the scars to prove it, but four eyes are better than two."

Cowan walked out into the street and paused there, glancing each way. He had his own back to watch, for Miller would be thinking of him first. But Ben was used to it—in his business the hunter was always the hunted as well.

He thought back to Cordelia Burton, and for a minute he felt a wistful longing, the yearning of a homeless man for a home and all that it can mean. He thought of how it would be to be sitting at a table with her across from him, the soft glow of lamplight on her face.

He shook his head, dismissing the thought. An officer of the law made little enough money . . . of course, a man could always file a homestead . . . and there was good range here in Arizona. He'd ridden over a pretty piece of it, time to time.

He had almost reached the Shoo-Fly, where he had left his bedroll, when he saw the shadows of two men on the ground before him. The rising moon had thrown their shadows on the street, otherwise he would have had no warning. Even as he glimpsed them, one shadow vanished and the other drew back close to the building.

Were they waiting for him? Had the other man gone around the building to take him from behind?

He hesitated a moment only, then turned on his heel and walked back to the saloon called the Hanging Wall, and went inside.

Several men loafed at the bar in desultory conversation, and there were three or four more around a table where a tired card game continued. One of these men looked around as he entered. It was Rio Bray.

Ben Cowan ordered a beer and waited. A moment passed, and then the door was pushed open and Miller came in. He started for the bar. His step faltered when he saw Ben Cowan, but he put his head down and came on, stopping a little distance away.

Miller leaned on the bar and pushed his hat back. Despite the cool night, he was suddenly perspiring. His eyes avoided Ben's. It was obvious that Miller had not suspected he was in the saloon.

Ben glanced down at his whiskey. Well, he wanted Miller, and there he was.

Why not take him now?

# CHAPTER 9

MILLER KNEW HIM, and the instant Ben started for him, Miller would be likely to draw a gun. Ben Cowan turned the idea over in his mind and decided to wait.

They stood not fifteen feet apart, with three other men between. Rio Bray had moved around to the other side of the table where he had been watching the card game, and stood now where he could keep an eye on Cowan.

Moreover, one of the men, sitting alone at a table, was Milton Duffield, an ex-U.S. Marshal, now a postal inspector, and a dangerous man with a gun. Duffield was a good man, with many local friends, but temperamental, and there was no certainty as to what he would do if a situation developed into gunplay. And he had been drinking heavily.

Ben Cowan suddenly remembered that his bedroll was back at the Shoo-Fly, and he had best retrieve it before the restaurant closed for the night.

Tucson at that time had no hotel. Those who had no friends in town bedded down wherever they could find a likely spot. There were a couple of abandoned houses used as camping spots by drifters—it was in one of these that Catlow had holed up. Word was passed on by word of mouth, and the houses were continually occupied by somebody. But most travelers bedded down in an empty corral or under a parked wagon.

Rio Bray strolled up and leaned on the bar beside Ben. "Howdy, Marshal! This here's a long way from the Cross Timbers."

Bray glanced down the bar at Miller. "Sure does beat all what a guilty conscience will do for a man, Marshal. Really starts a man sweating."

Miller's quick glance was filled with hatred, but Bray grinned back at him. "Better watch where you sleep, Marshal. Lots of folks around here are mighty careless where they leave their knives."

Miller put down his glass and went to the door. Ben Cowan watched him go, knowing that once outside Miller would dodge for shelter and probably wait for him to emerge.

"He ain't goin' no place tonight, Marshal," Bray said confidentially. "There's Apaches raiding around the country and Tucson's the safest place to be. Anyway, the Fifth Cavalry are going to give another band concert tomorrow night, and that's worth waitin' for."

Obviously Rio Bray had had more than a few drinks and was in a jovial, somewhat taunting mood. Ben was quite sure that Bray did not like him, and he felt no regret over that. Bray was a tough man and a good one, but a man who would have hit the outlaw trail sooner or later, regardless of circumstances.

"Yes, sir . . . a band concert! This town ain't no just ordinary town, Marshal. Why, just t'other day an *hombre* named Mansfield started himself a circulating library . . . got himself a whole stack of books to lend out!"

Rio Bray gulped his beer. "Why, this here's a regular metropolis! Now, I tell you—"

"Excuse me," Ben said abruptly, and turned swiftly to the door at the back.

He went through the short hall, then opened the door and stepped out into the darkness. Instantly, he moved to the right, and held still an instant to let his eyes grow accustomed to the darkness, all the while listening for the front door to close. Grimly, he reflected there was small chance of anybody going out that front door for a few minutes. Not if they suspected, as he did, that Miller was waiting out there.

Ben went around the corner of the building. The night was still. Somewhere, off beyond the town, a coyote yapped. The space next to the saloon was wide enough for a wagon to be standing there, a big freight wagon. He moved past it, his hand close to his gun. When he was half the length of the building he paused and studied what he could see of the street.

Opposite the saloon there was an adobe, the awning in front of it shielding the walk and most of the wall of the building in shadow. As he looked that way, something stirred behind him and he threw himself against the wagon on his left, drawing as he fell against it. He felt the whip of the bullet, then the thunderous roar of the shot between the walls of the two buildings. His answering fire was only an instant later, and he immediately ran toward the back, his pistol ready for a second shot.

All was dark and silent. He waited, listening, but

there was no sound; and then, from some distance off, somebody chuckled.

Ben Cowan hesitated, wanting to follow up that shot and find out who thought it was so funny, but his better judgment won and he went out into the street and made his way to the Shoo-Fly. With his bedroll he went through the alleys to the edge of town and bedded down there among some mesquite and cat-claw where he could not be approached without considerable noise.

It was daylight when he awakened.

Returning his bedroll to the Shoo-Fly, he ordered breakfast, and then went down the street to the back of the Hanging Wall.

He had no trouble finding the boot-prints of the man who had tried to kill him, for one of them was superimposed on his own track. Carefully, he worked out the trail.

Whoever had tried to kill him had not come around the building, *but had followed him from the saloon.*

He returned to the Shoo-Fly and his breakfast was brought to him. As he ate, he recalled man by man those who had been inside the Hanging Wall when he left through the back door. His memory for faces was good, but he could find no reason to suspect any particular man. Perhaps Miller had come back into the saloon as Ben left through the back.

He thought of Rio Bray, but dismissed the idea. Rio was close to Catlow, and Catlow would not want him killed . . . or would he?

Bray's random talk might have been simply the beer's effect, but it might have been more. Had Bray been holding him there for a reason?

"The trouble with you," Ben told himself, "is that you're suspicious of everybody."

But in his business a man had to be.

———

CORDELIA BURTON WAS up early, as was her habit. Her father was quiet, and left for his saddle shop earlier than usual. As she worked, her thoughts kept reverting not to Bijah Catlow, but to Ben Cowan.

She had never seen his face clearly, for it had always been shadowed by his hat brim, but she was sure she would know him if she saw him again, and curiously enough, she wanted to.

What sort of man was he? She was accustomed to quiet men, for a great many western men were quiet, not given to unnecessary talk. Was he really as sure of himself as he seemed?

"Mother," she said suddenly, "I'm going uptown."

Her mother glanced at her, mildly amused. "Bijah was here . . . before daylight."

"Bijah?"

"He must have been. I found this tucked under the back door."

Cordelia took the note, somehow less interested than she would have been a day earlier. She read:

*When I come back, you and me will have a talk.
If you need help, you go to Ben Cowan.*
                                            *Abijah*

He was gone, then. He had told her that he would be going one of these days, that he had some business in Mexico.

She would miss him, for nobody was more gay, more exciting, more full of fun . . . and yet, she reflected, there was no one to whom she would feel freer to go for help in case of trouble, the kind of trouble Miller could bring to herself and her family.

If she needed help, he said, she was to go to Ben Cowan. She remembered Bijah saying they had been friends since they were boys, and he had referred to Cowan with respect. Well, she needed no help, and she didn't need Ben Cowan. Nonetheless she found herself wondering what he looked like in broad daylight. You could learn little about a man from seeing only his chin and jawline. But there had been strength in that jaw, and a quiet strength in the way he talked.

It was excuse enough to go uptown, but it was not the excuse she used to her mother. Cordelia was nineteen, and at an age when most girls were married, and many already had families, but Cordelia was not to be stampeded into marriage. She had made up her own mind long since; if she did not find the man she wanted, she would settle for nothing less. Bijah had seemed to be the man, but she was not sure, and that was enough to warn her. In spite of all his good qualities, and they were many, there was a curious instability about Bijah Catlow that disturbed her.

Occasionally, he had spoken of owning a ranch, of buying cattle, of building something. He spoke of these things, yet they never seemed real to her coming from him, and she feared they were not real to him either. They represented what his better judgment told him he should do. Now, walking up the dusty street, she suddenly realized that Bijah might do none of the things he planned . . . he would do many things, but not those things . . . unless . . .

There was no sign of Ben Cowan on the street. From under her bonnet she kept her eyes busy as she walked. The usual loafers were along the Calle Real and the other streets she passed. Horses dozed at hitch rails, and here and there a freight wagon was discharging its load.

She stopped to talk to Mr. Kitchen, who ranched south of Tucson, about getting one of his hams. Pete Kitchen had tried large-scale farming in Arizona before anyone else, and was doing well, although occasionally his pigs sprouted so many Apache arrows that they were referred to as "Pete Kitchen's pincushions."

She ordered the ham, talked to Pete about General Allen's venture in bringing honeybees into Arizona, and kept her eyes busy. She would like to try keeping bees herself, she decided. Until General Allen brought his bees to Tucson early in 1872 all their honey had been brought up from Rancho Tia Juana, in Baja California.

She wanted to ask Pete if he had seen Ben Cowan, but she hesitated. Finally, after all her small talk, and just as she was turning away, she said, "Pete, have you seen that new United States Marshal who is around town?"

Pete nodded. "I saw him—he was headed south just after daybreak. He looked to me like a man with something on his mind."

Gone. . . . And he might not come back.

Kitchen glanced at her. "You worried about Catlow? That marshal ain't about to catch up to him."

"No . . . it isn't that. I—I had a message for him."

Pete turned away. "If he stops by my place, I'll tell him. I'm goin' back tonight."

Cordelia Burton turned toward home. What had Pete Kitchen meant when he said that the marshal was not going to catch up to Bijah? What would give Pete the idea that it was Bijah the marshal was following?

Obviously, it was a mistake, yet the thought disturbed her.

Ben Cowan had told her that Miller was his man, and Bijah had warned Miller about the marshal. Whatever Bijah knew that she did not, it had obviously frightened Miller into leaving, and for that both men deserved her gratitude.

Mentally, she began to go over that trail to the south. Every mile of it was dangerous, every mile had seen death by Apache warriors, every mile of it was liable to be raided at any time. Of all those who had tried to live to the south, only Pete Kitchen had survived any length of time, and his house and ranch were laid out for defense.

When she reached her own gate she went into the yard where her father had begun to plant grass for a lawn, and then paused as she looked back up the street. It was like her father, she thought, to bring his eastern ideas to Tucson, and to be among the first to plant trees, flowers, and grass with an idea of bringing coolness and beauty to the place.

Would Ben Cowan be like that? So many western men seemed heedless of anything but the present moment. She supposed it was because so few of them planned to stay wherever they were . . . or were too busy fighting Indians, drouth, and disaster to think of beauty.

She was undressing for bed when she heard General Allen come in. He often stopped by to talk with her father, and when she heard his voice she stopped to listen through the door, for he nearly always had news. And it was news he brought now.

". . . came in about ten minutes ago. That marshal had irons on Catlow. Threw him in jail."

There was an indistinct mumble, and then she heard the words, "wanted in Texas."

Bijah Catlow *arrested?*

# CHAPTER 10

B Y MORNING THE news was all over town—Bijah Catlow had been arrested. And then she discovered what everybody else seemed to know already . . . that Bijah Catlow was an outlaw and a gunfighter, known throughout the West.

Another story got around, too. Miller was wanted for desertion and murder, but he had vanished, dropped from sight as though he had never existed.

Soon everybody in Tucson was talking about the way Ben Cowan had taken Catlow, and it was Catlow himself who told the story, laughing at his own innocence in falling for an obvious trick.

He had been riding south through what seemed to be open country and there, lying in the trail ahead of him was a brand-new white sombrero, obviously expensive. Intrigued, Catlow dismounted and bent over to pick up the hat, and from behind him Ben Cowan ordered him to hold his position.

Bent over as he was, his pistol riding around in front of his hip, his body would impede any attempt at a draw; and to straighten, draw, and turn was too much of a chance against a man as fast as Ben Cowan. Catlow surrendered.

Ben Cowan slipped the cuffs on him. "I don't want to kill you, Bijah," he explained, "and damned if I don't think you'd try to make a break."

"Sure as hell would!" Bijah said ruefully. "I got business below the border."

Ben Cowan did not talk about the capture, but Catlow was full of the story, and it passed from person to person around the stables and the saloons, that Ben Cowan had outsmarted his old friend, lying hidden in a shallow place that apparently would not hide a desert fox, waiting until Catlow bent over to pick up the hat.

It made a good story, and Ben Cowan found himself suddenly a popular man, doubly so as it was obvious that Catlow, who was well-liked, held no grudge.

Cowan was sitting at his desk working over a report when Cordelia Burton appeared with a basket covered with a napkin.

"Marshal Cowan? May I give this to the prisoner?"

He looked at her gravely. "I will have to look it over."

She stiffened indignantly. "You do not trust me?"

"Ma'am, where Bijah is concerned I trust nobody. That man is wily as a snake and trickier than a 'coon."

He rummaged through the basket, his mouth watering as he saw half an apple pie, a large breast of chicken, and other assorted edibles.

Bijah Catlow got up from his cot and came to the bars, his face flushed a deep red. "Ma'am, I sure never calculated to have you see me in such a place."

"Then you shouldn't have done whatever it was you did to get in here. I am sure the marshal had reason for arresting you."

"Oh, sure! He had reason, all right!" He grinned

his appreciation. "Where d'you suppose he got the idea for that durned hat trick? I never heard of such a thing! There was that brand-new hat lyin' there in the trail and nobody around, nowhere. Seemed like somebody had lost a good hat. Then just as I bent to pick it up, he had me."

"You like him, don't you?"

Bijah glanced at her quickly. "Ben? Best man I ever did know." He looked at her with a grin. "But you just wait . . . see who has the last laugh."

The town had it the next morning, for Bijah Catlow was gone.

Ben Cowan had stayed on watch until almost daylight, then had unrolled his bed and turned in.

An hour later the jailer shook Ben awake. "He's gone! Catlow's took out!"

The cell was empty.

The jailer's story was simple. He was making coffee when his daughter appeared at the door. He opened it and she came in, followed by three masked men. They had gagged and bound him and his daughter, taken the keys from him, and opened the cell to let Catlow out.

She had not been molested in any way. In fact, aside from threatening her with the gun, they had treated her with utmost politeness.

Knowing Bijah and how well-liked he was among the Spanish-speaking population, Ben Cowan suspected the jailer's daughter had been only too willing to cooperate, and the gun a mere gesture. The jailer himself did not seem very disturbed by the escape.

In disgust, Ben Cowan tore up the report of Catlow's capture and headed for the stable for his horse.

The horse was gone. Tacked to the side of the stall was a note.

You can pick him up at Pete Kitchen's. Sorry to set you afoot, but I got business to attend to.

There was no signature, and no need for one, but within the hour Ben Cowan realized just how many friends Catlow had, and how important they could be, for nobody in town had a horse that was ready to go. Either they had just gone lame, or they had been promised, or they were out at pasture, or somehow indisposed.

By afternoon several people came to him offering horses, but they knew and he knew that by that time Bijah Catlow was gone beyond recapture, and the town of Tucson was chuckling again.

Ben Cowan sat behind the scarred desk in the jail office and considered the situation. Bijah Catlow, and Miller as well—both had eluded him.

Bijah Catlow had undoubtedly gone to Mexico. Ben Cowan considered the probabilities and decided that Miller had gone the same way. He was a deserter, although his time in the Army had been of brief duration, and possibly only for the chance to watch the paymaster. He must avoid places where he might be recognized. His stop in Tucson was probably en route to Mexico, anyway.

Bijah Catlow had spoken of a big strike. Allowing for exaggeration, what were his chances in Sonora or Chihuahua, both within riding distance? Carefully, Ben considered the possibilities, but they were few and none seemed to promise anything like the amount of money Catlow must have had in mind, from the way he talked and planned.

The arrival of the Mexican soldier was obviously tied in with his plan. Had it then, anything to do with the Mexican army? A payroll, perhaps? Or captured loot?

With no idea of what way to take, Ben Cowan began in the only way he knew how: he began by asking questions, by starting a conversation in the direction he wished it to go, and then just listening. What he wanted to know about was Mexico.

The hint that he needed came from Allen. They were talking over lunch at the Palace—the Shoo-Fly's only rival in Tucson—and Allen was commenting on the death of Juarez and the succession of Lerdo to the presidency.

"You know," Allen said, "I have been expecting this would happen, and wondering if when it happened that silver would turn up."

"Silver?"

"Sebastian Lerdo de Tejada was the strong right arm of Juarez during some trying times, and before the French intervention both the Conservatives and the Liberals were in desperate need of money. The simplest way to get it was to confiscate some of the shipments from the mines, and Lerdo moved swiftly. One of those shipments had just been seized when, on June 10th, 1863, General Forey, with 30,000 French soldiers, entered the City of Mexico.

"Juarez fled to San Luis Potosì, and the mule train loaded with two million dollars in silver and gold vanished from sight. Yet in 1867 when Juarez was elected president and Lerdo was in his cabinet, there was already a somewhat reserved feeling between them. Later, Lerdo ran against Juarez for the presidency, was defeated, but became president of the Supreme Court; and on the death of Juarez, Lerdo became president."

"What about the two millions in silver?"

"Some of that two millions was in gold. Well, nobody who knows the whole story will tell it; but Lerdo had ambitions of his own, and apparently kept the knowledge of that treasure to himself, holding it back against such a time as has now come. He is president, and such a treasure would be of enormous use to him—especially with such a formidable rival as Diaz."

Ben Cowan listened as Allen talked on, discussing the involved politics of the land below the border in that year of 1872.

Tucson, in many respects, had closer ties with Mexico than with the United States. Only a few years earlier it had in fact been a part of Mexico, and many of the local population had been citizens of Mexico and had relatives there. Many of the local Anglos had married girls of Spanish descent, and were vitally concerned with Mexican affairs.

Suppose . . . just suppose . . . that Lerdo had removed those two millions from their hiding place and was having it transferred to Mexico City?

The possibility was slight, but the chance was there . . . depending on where that silver actually was . . . and that Mexican soldier could have been a messenger to Catlow.

"That silver—would it have been somewhere in Sonora when it disappeared?"

"You've heard the story then? Yes, as a matter of fact, it was. And it dropped right out of sight. But you can take it from me that if anyone knows where it was, Lerdo is the man. He's a deep one. Brilliant man," Allen commented; "shrewd, capable, and yet I do not believe he understands the temper of his people. He has lived too far from them, I think."

Later that night Ben Cowan loitered at the bar of the Quartz Rock Saloon. He listened to the talk around him but said nothing himself; when the moment came, he spoke quietly to the bartender. "There was a Mex soldier in here . . . stranger in town . . . stopped around here and the Hanging Wall, talked to Bijah Catlow some. I'd be interested to know what they talked about."

The bartender hesitated, then met Ben's gaze with cool, searching eyes. "Bijah is a friend of mine. I'd heard he was a friend of yours . . . and then you jugged him."

"Look"—Ben spoke softly—"Bijah is a friend of mine, but he's so damned bullheaded he won't listen to a friend, and he's walking himself right into a trap."

Cowan knew he was stretching things a bit, but he felt that what he was saying might be true.

"He's tackled something too big for him, and he's going to get killed unless I can stop him—and I don't even know where he's gone. After all," he added, "I couldn't arrest him in Mexico, anyway."

"Yeah," the bartender agreed, "that's so."

He served a beer down the bar, then came back to Ben. "I got no idea where they went—only that Mex, I heard him mention Hermosillo a couple of times . . . and something about a mule train. I think," he went on, "he was trying to sell Bijah on the idea that whatever they did had to be done before that mule train reached Hermosillo."

It was little enough, but Ben Cowan had pieced a trail together on much less. Still, he had no authority in Mexico, and at the moment there was little good feeling between the two countries . . . although Washington, and the United States Marshal's office in particular, had instructed him to do all he could to promote good feeling with Mexican officials.

If it was true—and he had no evidence at all on which to proceed—that Catlow had gone into Mexico to attempt to steal the two million in treasure long concealed by President Lerdo, then he must be stopped. Such a theft by American bandits, if successful, would deal a serious blow to all future relations with Mexico. Ben Cowan knew what the cooperation of Mexican officials could mean, as did his superiors.

All right, then. The chances were good that Bijah Catlow had gone to Hermosillo. So Ben Cowan would go there too, trying all the way to pick up the trail he wanted. Fortunately, a man as flamboyant as Catlow would not be difficult to follow.

———

FOR DAYS BEFORE Catlow left, Ben had been preparing for a trip. He had bought a pack horse, had purchased supplies and extra ammunition, and while talking with people about the town, he had listened to much discussion of trails into Mexico.

"The Apaches are the danger," somebody had commented. "When they raid they go in small bands so they have no need to hold to the trails where the water holes are. Why, out there in the desert there are seeps and hidden tanks in the rocks with water a-plenty—a-plenty for six or seven men, maybe even a dozen if the water isn't used too often."

Several days had passed since Catlow escaped jail, and Cowan had done nothing. It seemed that he had no plans to do anything. And then, suddenly, he was gone.

Cordelia Burton saw Ben on his last day in town. He was standing on the street nearby when she emerged from her father's shop. She hesitated, and regarded him thoughtfully.

He was a remarkably handsome man, when one took time to look at him, and she liked the easy, casual way he handled his tall, lean body. His face was lean, browned by sun and honed by wind, and there was something about his eyes, something that haunted her, but she could not decide what it was. She should have asked Bijah about him, she thought.

He straightened up when he saw her, and removed his hat. His dark brown hair was curly; now it showed distinct reddish tones that she had not seen before.

He fell into step beside her. "I haven't much excuse to walk you home," he said, ". . . not in broad daylight."

"Do you need an excuse?"

He smiled slightly, and laugh wrinkles at the corners of his eyes broke the gravity of his expression. "No, ma'am, I guess I don't." He glanced at her again. "Have you heard from Bijah?"

"No."

"He's going to be a hard man to take." He paused a moment. "You ever lived on a ranch, ma'am?"

"No . . . not exactly. It seems a lonely life."

"Depends . . . there's plenty to do. I take kindly to open lands. I like to look far off. Seems like a man's free, whether he is or not."

"You do not think a man can be free?"

"No, ma'am, not exactly. Maybe . . . some ways. There's always his duty, duty to folks about him, to his country, to the law . . . such-like."

She looked at him thoughtfully, then stood still so she could see his face well. "Ben, you believe in your duty, don't you?"

He shrugged slightly, and squinted his eyes against the sun. It might be that he was embarrassed to speak of such a thing. "Without duty, life don't make any kind of sense, ma'am. If folks are going to live together they have to abide by some kind of rules, and the law is those rules. The law doesn't work against a man, it works for him. Without it, every house would have to be a fortress, and no man or woman would be safe. First time two men got together I expect they started to make laws for living together.

"There's always mavericks who can't or won't ride a straight trail, and the law needs somebody to ride herd on them."

"And you are one of the herders?"

"Sort of." He smiled. "I need some herding myself, time to time."

He looked down at her. "Living on a ranch mightn't be as bad as you think," he said.

At sunup the next morning he was ten miles south of town and riding for the border.

He had a man to take . . . two of them, as a matter of fact.

# CHAPTER 11

BIJAH CATLOW HAD entered Mexico and disappeared.

So far as Ben Cowan could discover there had been only four men in the group. One of these, judging by descriptions, was Old Man Merridew, and a second would surely be Rio Bray. As the fourth man was a Mexican, it was probably the soldier who had met Bijah in Tucson.

Whatever Catlow planned could scarcely be done by so small a group, so Ben Cowan loitered about Nogales on both sides of the border, and bought quite a few drinks, and asked quite a few questions. Had there been any other strange gringos in town that night? Gringos who were no longer around?

There had been—two, at least. They had ridden off on the trail toward Magdalena . . . a very foolish thing to do, for the Apaches made travel along that trail much too dangerous, except for large, well-armed groups.

To the click of castanets, the rattle of glasses, and the somber singing of a Mexican girl, Ben Cowan leaned on the bar and listened. He bought tequila, and he drank it, but most of the time he made idle talk in his fluent cow-country Spanish—and as always, he listened.

Wherever people gather together, they talk, and

often they talk too much. In towns where there is little news and little else but one's surroundings to discuss, they invariably talk too much.

When Ben Cowan rode from Nogales down the Magdalena trail, he rode alone, and soon he picked up the hoofprints left by the horses of Catlow, Bray, and Merridew. He had quickly become familiar with these around Tucson.

Others had left Tucson after them, but he could follow the tracks of Catlow's men with much difficulty. When they seemed to disappear from the trail he turned about and rode back. The trail had been almost obliterated by a herd of goats—undoubtedly not an accident—but soon the goats had turned toward Nogales and the four had ridden on.

Ben Cowan found where they had camped that first night in an arroyo only a few miles southwest of Nogales. Two other riders joined them there, and the party of six rode on.

A half-day's ride farther along, an Indian had joined them, an unmounted Indian. Ben back-trailed that Indian and found where he had waited a couple of hundred yards off the trail, smoking dozens of cigarettes and evidently watching for Catlow. When the party continued on, the Indian trotted beside Catlow's horse.

Now, a man who rides in wild country devotes quite as much time to his back trail as to that ahead, not only because he may be followed, but because he may have to retrace his steps, and the back trail does not look the same to him. Many a traveler has failed to watch his back trail and, turning back, has found nothing familiar in the country over which he has traveled, and becomes lost.

Ben Cowan, who had been holding to low ground for the most part, and riding parallel to the route the others were taking, now discovered that somebody else was following them . . . or him. A solitary rider and what appeared to be a black horse.

That lone rider raised no dust, so the chances were that Ben himself raised none, yet the rider must know of his presence, for from time to time his own trail had joined that of Catlow's band.

On the fourth day of riding, Cowan came to several decisions. The first was that the other man trailing them must be Miller; and another was that the Indian trotting beside Catlow must be a Tarahumara, one of a tribe noted for their tremendous faculty for endurance. A Tarahumara who could not run a hundred miles was scarcely worthy of belonging to the tribe—though as far as that went, the Apaches were great runners and walkers, men who preferred to fight on their feet, rarely on horseback.

Also, Catlow was looking for something in country with which he was not familiar. That Indian, Ben knew, had been brought along for the purpose of leading them to the little-known seeps, water holes, and rock tanks. There were many of those to be found in the desert, but they were rarely used because they were known only to wild things, including a few wild Indians. They held little water, not enough for any but a small party, sometimes scarcely enough for more than one or two men.

But by following such a route Catlow would be able to penetrate deep into Sonora without being seen or questioned. It was a shrewd idea, and it indicated that Catlow had planned better than was his usual method. This was something to be remembered . . . Bijah Catlow was thinking, and Bijah was shrewd, with a brilliant imagination. Knowing all the tricks, he was capable of coming up with a few new ones on the spur of the moment.

The route presented an acute problem for Ben Cowan as well. Most of the water holes the men used would be exhausted before he reached them . . . in fact, Catlow no doubt depended on that very fact to eliminate pursuit.

That night five more riders joined Catlow. Rather, the five were waiting when Catlow and his men came. This, then, was what he had been looking for, and he had not been exactly sure where their camp would be.

An hour after daybreak Ben Cowan came up to the camp. His canteen had less than a pint of water in it, and his horse was desperate for a drink. And the bottom of the small seep where their camp had been was simply a few feet of drying mud.

There was no question of going on. First, he must have water, for the next water hole might be even worse. With a discarded tin can, Ben dropped to his knees and in a few minutes had scooped out a deep hole in the center of the mud. He worked a little longer, then withdrew to the shade, and settled down to wait.

Water might seep in . . . if it did not, he would have to strike out for the main trail and hope that he reached it at a point not too far from water.

He thought Catlow was headed for Hermosillo, but he did not know. Their destination might be

Altar, not far off now; or, more likely, Magdalena and its rich mines. He could only find out by staying with Catlow and his band.

It was noon before he allowed his horse to drink, and shadows were gathering before he could fill his canteen. There was no possibility of keeping up with their trail in the dark, but a few hours of daylight remained, and there was the man following him to consider.

If he was still back there, he would come up with this seep in the same condition Ben Cowan had found it in, and he would undoubtedly make camp there. During the night Cowan might elude him.

Ben saddled up and rode out of the hollow where the seep lay, holding to low ground as much as possible, and wary of an ambush. But Miller was no longer first in his mind; he hoped above all to prevent Catlow from carrying out whatever it was he had planned.

He picked up the trail and rode away at a canter, making several quick changes of direction in case his follower was taking a sight at him, or circling to head him off. When darkness finally came, he took a last sight along the line of tracks he followed, lining them up with a mountain peak that would be visible for some time after nightfall. The great risk lay in the party he pursued veering off toward another water hole that lay to the east or west, in which case he would lose them, and the water as well.

He slacked off on the reins, trusting to the horse. The roan was desert- and mountain-bred, accustomed to dry, rocky wastelands, and it would naturally go toward water. Moreover, the horse knew he was following a party of mounted men, and wild horses have been known to follow a scent as well as any hound.

For two hours the roan walked steadily toward the south; when it veered sharply off, he permitted it to go, only pausing from time to time to listen. The slightest noise carries far in the silence of a desert night, and he neither wanted to come on the others unexpectedly, or to betray his own presence by noise.

Suddenly, his horse stopped. Ben gathered the reins, listening into the night. He heard no sound.

They had paused in the deep shadow of a sheer wall of rock that reared up from the desert sand. About him was scattered brush. It was cooler in the shadow of the rock, and he waited, but the roan showed no disposition to move on.

He walked the horse closer to the rock face and dismounted. Judging by the actions of his horse, there was water near, but the roan had not gone up to it, so it was probably beyond reach.

Stripping the rig from the tired animal, he picketed the roan on a small patch of grass, then he dug into his saddlebag for a piece of jerked beef. After a while, when the sky was spangled with stars, he rolled up in his blankets and slept.

Far off, a coyote howled . . . a quail called its question into the night, and above the horse and man the black cliff leaned, somber and stark against the blue-black sky.

He awakened suddenly in the cool dim light just before the dawn. His first glance was to his horse, for the roan was erect, ears up, nostrils flared. Swiftly, Ben was beside the horse, whispering a warning, putting a hand to its nostrils to stifle a whinny.

After a moment of silence he heard the steps of a walking horse. A horse that walked, paused . . . then came on again.

Ben Cowan shot a quick glance at his Winchester and gun-belt which lay on his ground-sheet beside the blankets. He wanted those guns desperately, but feared the sounds the move would make, and he did not dare to leave the horse. Something beyond the mere coming of a strange horse seemed to have alarmed the roan.

Suddenly, on a low rise off to his left, he saw the horse. Even as he glimpsed it, the animal let out a questioning whinny. The small breeze was from the strange horse and toward them, but it must have realized the presence of another horse.

The animal came a step nearer . . . there was something on its back . . . something more than a saddle. A pack? The shape was wrong.

It was a man, slumped down. A man wounded or in trouble of some kind.

Waiting no longer, Ben Cowan stepped quickly to his gun-belt and slung it about his hips, slipping the thong from his six-shooter as he did so.

Then, leaving his own horse, he walked toward the strange animal, talking in a low, friendly tone. The horse took a step or two nearer, hesitant and anxious, as if wanting the presence of a human.

Ben paused, listening. Never unaware of danger, he lived always with the possibility of it, and no amount of easy living would ever take this from him. He was born to it, and was glad of it. He listened, but he heard nothing but the breathing of the horse.

He went up to the animal. A man lay slumped

upon its back, tied in place crudely but efficiently. Ben led the horse to his camp and, having untied the knots, he lifted the wounded man from the saddle.

He was a Mexican officer in uniform, shot in the body and the leg. Hesitating only briefly at taking the risk, Ben dismissed it as one that must be taken, and put together a small fire. He built it close against the cliff and under a smoke tree where the rising smoke would be spread out and dissipated by even that sparse foliage—if such it could be called.

There was little water in his canteen, but he put a part of it on to boil; then he slipped off the wounded man's coat and split his pants leg. The bullet in the body had gone through flesh above the hip and had bled badly. The bullet hole in the leg seemed to have touched no bone, but the wounded man had lost blood there, too.

When the water was hot, Ben bathed the wounds and bound them up with the matadura herb. He had no powder, nor was it possible to prepare any, but he used the herb just as he had found it.

When he had finished dawn had come, and he sat back on the ground and looked around him.

He had to have water, and water must be close by, for he doubted if the roan would have stopped for any other reason. He glanced up at the rock wall. There could be a rock tank up there, a *tinaja,* as the Mexicans called it, a natural hollow where water from the scarce rains might be found.

He got to his feet. And then for the first time he had a good look at the horse the man had been riding.

It was Miller's horse.

# CHAPTER 12

THE YOUNG OFFICER lay still, but his breathing seemed less ragged and harsh. He was a handsome man, but now, in the early light, he looked pale, drained of blood by his wounds.

Ben knew that the wounded man would awaken to a raging thirst, and there was scarcely a cup of water remaining in Ben's canteen. Under the circumstances, there was nothing to do but leave him and go in search of water.

Taking up his rifle and canteen, he walked northward along the wall of rock. It was a sheer wall for at least forty feet up, then it seemed to break back and rise up farther, jagged and serrated. It was perhaps two hundred feet above the desert floor at its highest, which was to the south of him. If there was any way to get up into those rocks, it must be from the end, or from the other side.

The ridge was all of three hundred yards long. When he reached the end of it, it appeared to be no more than a third of that in width, but there was plenty of room up there for a tank. However, knowing such places as he did, Ben Cowan knew that without some clue he might die of thirst trying to find the water.

He studied the sand for animal tracks, but found none. A bee flew past, pointing away on a straight line of flight into the rocks, and he followed, taking a sight on a pinnacle of rock. He lost the bee, but went on for several yards in the direction of its flight, and then stopped.

The sun would soon be fully up, and the pale light of morning lay all about. Here and there were shadows among the rocks of the ridge. Glancing back toward camp, he could see the horses with their heads turned toward him, watching him. After a moment, they returned to their cropping of the dusty brown grass or brush.

Another bee passed, but he lost it. He walked on up among the rocks and found the track of a coyote or desert fox. . . . It was smudged somewhat and he could not make out which it was. The animal had gone on up into the rocks, and Ben scrambled over the rocks and climbed higher.

By the time he was well up into the rocks the sun was up and already hot. He climbed a shoulder of granite and studied the surroundings with care. He saw nothing green, nothing to indicate water.

The rocks about him were dull red, except off to the left where an upthrust of granite partly blocked his view. Sand had blown into the crevices, but as he climbed there was less of this. Brush grew here and there, sparse gray, unlikely-looking stuff that promised nothing. Here he must depend on chance, on what he knew about rock tanks, and what the wildlife, if any, indicated.

He clambered on. Sweat trickled down his face, the empty canteen battered against the rocks. He stopped again, his gaze sweeping the surrounding country. In every direction there was desert . . . greasewood, cactus. His searching eyes found nothing to promise water.

Suddenly a bee went past him, so swiftly that he lost it instantly. He started on again, but where he climbed there was no easy way, no game trail, no way found by Indians. The coyote whose tracks he had seen earlier had not come this way; it must have turned off through some crevice or around some boulder.

He was high above the desert now. Searching for a way to proceed, he saw a flat-topped boulder whose edge he could reach with his fingers. Being a cautious man, he picked up a pebble and flipped it up. If a snake was lying there, it would surely be aroused and rattle. He had no desire to pull himself over that edge and come face to face with a rattler. He flipped another pebble, but nothing happened.

He pulled himself up and looked over a maze of dark rocks, smooth with the varnish of the desert. He got to his feet and looked back down the way he had come.

The picketed horses fed on the brush, but the wounded man was too close to the rock face to be seen from here. Ben climbed a little way over the rocks and suddenly, in a small patch of blown sand, he saw the edge of a track . . . a porcupine track. From the rocks ahead, a bird flew up.

Turning that way, he found himself on a narrow path, scarcely wide enough to place one foot ahead of the other between the rocks. Ahead, a huge boulder blocked the view, but when he rounded it he saw a deep, dark pool of water.

Lifting his eyes, he saw another pool, slightly

higher and just beyond it. Here the runoff from the highest part of the rocks was caught in the natural basins and held there.

The upper pool, which was the easier to reach, was half-shadowed by an overhang of rock. The water was cold, very cold, and sweet. He drank, then drank again and filled his canteen.

He looked down at the lower pool. Bees clustered around it, and he saw at the edge the droppings of a deer or mountain sheep—at this distance he could not make out which.

Following the path back, he found a comparatively easy route, and was quickly down to the desert floor.

The horses whinnied as he approached. The wounded man was conscious, and stared wildly at Ben as he approached.

"What happened?" he asked in Spanish. "Who are you?"

Ben Cowan squatted on his heels, and offered the wounded man a drink. Then he told him, as briefly as possible, what the situation was. "First off," he said finally, "I've got to get those horses to water or they'll break loose and go by themselves."

The wounded Mexican looked up at him. "Have you a gun? If you can spare me one, I'll be all right." He paused. "You know, of course, that this is Apache country?"

"I know."

"Each minute you stay with me you risk your life, señor."

Ben Cowan got his spare Colt from the saddlebag. "Take this," he said, "but don't shoot unless you have to. I'll be keeping a lookout from up above."

When he returned from watering the horses, the Mexican had managed to move and had dragged his bed deeper into the narrowing shadow of the cliff.

"Now you tell me," Cowan said to him, "where you got that horse."

Captain Diego Martinez de Recalde shrugged. "We were riding from Fronteras to Magdalena," he explained, "and as I was going home to Guadalajara, I took with me my very special horse. I was trying his paces some distance from the column when I thought I saw a horse standing alone on the desert.

"I rode closer to see . . . something hit me and I fell, hearing the shot as I struck the ground. A man rode up to me, shot at me again, and I remember nothing more."

"He shot you for your horse," Cowan said. "His own wasn't much good and was about played out."

"You know him, señor?"

"I know him . . . he's one of the reasons I am in Mexico. If I can arrange to take him here, I would like to take him back with me."

Recalde smiled, somewhat grimly. "You shall have every assistance, señor. I promise it. However," he added, "if he rides that horse where any of my command see him, I fear you shall not have much to take back."

After Ben had dressed the wound again, he brought up the subject of travel. Captain Recalde agreed with him at once. Difficult, even dangerous as it might be for Recalde to travel, to remain where he was would be even more dangerous. And by this time his soldiers would be searching for him.

Ben Cowan helped Recalde into the saddle and

mounted up. There was no longer any question of attempting to trail either Miller or Catlow. Now he must get the wounded man to his own column of soldiers, marching southward, and then he could ride with them into Hermosillo, or at least to Magdalena.

Recalde was gripping the pommel with both hands. "It is not a way to ride, señor," he said, "but—"

"You stay in that saddle any way you can," Ben responded, "and don't worry about how."

The desert was like an oven. Above them in the brassy sky there floated an enormous sun, a sun that seemed to encompass the entire heavens. Steadily they rode southward, south by east, hoping to come upon the trail.

Their walking horses plodded through the sand interminably; their slow advance was broken only by the moments when they stopped for Recalde to drink. The sun was high above, and the desert all around them danced with heat waves. Ben's clothes were stiff with dust and sweat, and sweat trickled down his spine and down his chest under his shirt.

His rifle barrel he sheathed, for it became too hot to hold. White dust rose from the desert, a soft white dust that clung and choked. The wounded man rode with head bowed, his fingers clinging to the pommel, his body swaying loosely with the movements of the horse.

The afternoon came; the brassy sun still hung in the sky. The day seemed to go on forever. Once Recalde's horse stumbled, and seemed about to fall. They pushed on . . . and then they came upon the trail. It was empty of life.

Tracks were there, tracks of wagons and of

mounted men, tracks several hours old. They had, evidently, reached the trail some distance behind the column . . . at this point the Captain's disappearance would not yet have been discovered.

Recalde's horse stumbled again, and had Cowan not thrown out a quick arm, the Captain would have fallen. The horse stood, legs spread, head hanging.

Alone, without a rider, the horse might make it through. Mounted, neither the horse nor the wounded man could make it.

Ben Cowan swung down and helped Recalde, who was no longer aware of his surroundings, into his own saddle. Leaving the other horse behind, he started off, leading his roan.

Slowly, the long day waned. Shadows began to gather behind the shrubs and the rocks here and there along the trail. Ahead of them there seemed to be a small range of mountains, or a ridge of rocks.

Ben Cowan thought no more of time, he thought only of coolness, of shadow, of night, of water. What remained in the canteen, the wounded man would need.

They were stupid with heat and weariness, and they did not hear the hoofbeats muffled by dust. The four riders came upon them suddenly, no less surprised than Cowan; until that moment desert growth had masked their coming.

Four Apaches . . . not over sixty feet away.

Ben Cowan saw them and drew. He did not think, for he was at that moment beyond thought. This was danger, and his life had been geared to danger. He drew, and the speed of his hand was his margin of safety. The gun cleared his holster and the bullet ripped into the chest of the nearest Indian.

Completely surprised, the others broke for shelter, and Ben Cowan jerked the horse behind the nearby rocks. Reaching up, he took Recalde bodily from the saddle just as a bullet cut a notch in the cantle.

He dropped Recalde and swung the muzzle of his pistol, blasting into the nearest bit of brush. Leaping away from Recalde, he crouched down behind the clustering rocks, and snapped a shot at a brown arm—and missed.

Bullets flaked rock from near his head. One man was there . . . two would be circling him, and he had no defense from behind.

Then a bullet killed the roan. The horse lunged forward and fell, and Ben Cowan swore bitterly, for that had been a good horse, perhaps the best horse he had ever owned.

Ben turned at the shot, and was in time to see the Apache duck to change positions, and this time he did not miss. The Apache stumbled and plunged to his face in the sand, and Ben Cowan put another bullet into him as he hit the ground.

Rock chips stung his face. He glanced toward Recalde. The Mexican had come out of it; feebly he was trying to get at the Colt in his waistband. Dampness stained his coat and shirt . . . he was bleeding again.

There were no more shots. The Apaches knew night was coming, and they knew he wasn't going anywhere without a horse. They could wait . . . and he shot too well.

Ben Cowan crawled to Recalde, got his left arm under the Mexican's shoulders, and pulled him close behind the rocks. Then he clutched at slabs of rock and took them to build quickly a low, crude barricade around them. He reloaded his pistol, and got his rifle.

When darkness came the Indians might come for him; or more likely—for no Apache liked night-fighting—they would wait until daybreak and take him when he was dead for sleep. They had him, and they knew it.

Diego Recalde looked at him with pain-filled eyes. "I have killed you, señor," he said. "I ask forgiveness, I ask it in the name of God."

"Everybody dies," Ben Cowan said. "If not this way, another. But if it is forgiveness you want, you have it."

He looked up at the sky. The sun was gone. At least, he thought, death would be cool.

# CHAPTER 13

H E CHECKED THE action of his rifle, wiping it carefully clean with his bandana. There were at least two Indians out there, and others might have joined them, drawn by the shooting. There could be no thought of sleep, for Recalde was in no shape to take over the guard for even a part of the night.

Cowan not only knew that the Apache does not like to fight during the hours of night, but he knew why. It is the Apache's belief that if a man is killed in darkness his soul must forever wander, homeless and alone; but the love of loot can overcome even superstition, and there might be an unbeliever among these Apaches.

Moving with infinite care, he got several stones and eased them into place among the rocks to make a better barricade. As he slipped the last stone into its notch a bullet smashed against the rock, spattering him with a hail of stinging stone fragments. Then it was quiet again.

The last light faded, stars appeared, and the face of the desert became cool. His canteen with its small bit of water was tied to his saddle, but the dying horse had fallen upon it. For all the good it could be to them, it might have been a mile away.

The long night began. Recalde awoke, and the two men talked occasionally in whispers. Weariness lay heavily upon Ben Cowan, and he fought to keep his eyes open. He tried to moisten his cracked and bloody lips, but his tongue was like a stick in his mouth, for he had drunk little of the water, saving most of it for the wounded man. It was with an effort that he could make himself heard when he spoke.

Where was Catlow now, he wondered. Far to the south of him, no doubt, and not even aware that Ben was in Mexico.

And what would Cordelia Burton be doing now? He thought of her cool, quiet beauty, of the kind of wistful assurance that was so much a part of her. Bijah Catlow was a fool to be risking his neck in Mexico, with such a girl waiting for him back in Tucson.

Through the night Recalde's muttering became disconnected; he talked of his home, of his father and mother, of his sisters. His head twisted from side to side, and once he cried out in the night.

At last day came with a feeble grayness over the far-off Sierra Madre . . . the fainter stars vanished, and the few bright ones faded—all but one, which hung alone long after the others had gone. His eyes red-rimmed from heat, dust, and exhaustion, Ben Cowan waited for what was to come, staring around him.

Recalde was sleeping . . . well, let him sleep then. If he was lucky, he would never wake.

They came out of the gray dawning like rolling clumps of tumbleweed, so swiftly and silently that at first he thought his eyes deceived him. Their feet made scarcely a whisper in the soft sand, and they ran bent far over to offer little target.

More had come up during the night . . . how many were there? Six? Eight?

They had not taken a dozen strides before his six-gun shattered the silence with its long, deadly roll of unbroken sound. Slip-shooting, he emptied the gun with no break in the roar of sound, then dropped the gun and caught up his Winchester.

Two Apaches were down . . . another was dragging a leg, seeking shelter. Cowan dropped the Winchester muzzle on the nearest man's chest and squeezed off his shot; then he turned and fired without lifting the butt to his shoulder, and saw another spin half around.

Recalde came up on one elbow, firing.

An Apache sprang over the rock barrier and Ben Cowan struck with the rifle butt, holding the rifle shoulder high. He heard the bones in the man's face crunch, and then he whipped the rifle around and shot into another—a running Indian.

*Running?*

With a thunder of hoofs, a cavalry detachment swept by their little fort, guns blasting. Even as the fleeing Apache neared the brush a saber cut him down, chopping through his skull to his eyebrows, so that the soldier had to put a foot on the Apache's shoulder to wrench the blade free.

Recalde caught a rock and pulled himself erect, clinging to its top. "Señor!" he shouted. "I told you they would come! It is my soldier! My *compadres*!"

———

GENERAL JUAN BAUTISTA Armijo smiled tolerantly. "I thank you, my friend, but what you suggest is impossible. No such treasure is known to me, and even if it were, our soldiers would make theft impossible."

Ben Cowan spoke again. "Señor, I do not wish to dispute you, but I have information that two million in silver and gold are to be moved from its hiding place and transferred to Mexico City, by order of the President himself."

The General's expression was unyielding, but his eyes were not unfriendly. "I am sorry, señor. Such is not the case." He paused. "I should be most curious to know the source of such a story."

"It is a rumor, and only that." Briefly, Ben Cowan outlined the story, and coupled it with Catlow's boast and the appearance and disappearance of the Mexican soldier. Yet even as he repeated it, he realized on what a flimsy basis he had constructed his theory. He felt a little ashamed, for there could be no doubt that the basis of the story was weak.

"I am sorry, señor," Armijo repeated, "but I do thank you for your interest. I also wish to extend our thanks for saving the life of my brother-in-law."

"I do, however, have your permission to search for Señor Catlow and those with him? And to arrest them if I find them?"

The General waved his hand. "Of course! We have thieves enough of our own without wishing to keep any of yours. Take him, and welcome! If there is any way in which we can assist you, you have only to call on us."

When they were outside, Recalde shrugged a shoulder. "You see? I was sure he would not believe you, and as for the treasure—"

"He knew about the treasure."

Recalde looked at him skeptically. "Do you think so? He seemed amused by the amount. After all, *amigo,* two million dollars—it is a very great deal."

"He would have been a fool to even hint at it. After all, there are plenty of men in Mexico who would not hesitate to try to steal that much. The fewer who know the better."

"This man, this Catlow . . . you know him well, then?"

Cowan explained as best he could the strange relationship between himself and Catlow: never quite friends, never quite enemies; always a respect, each for the other.

Recalde listened, his pale face attentive. He nodded at last. "I see . . . it is, ah—delicate." He glanced at Cowan. "He may kill you, señor. He may, indeed." And then he added, "Or you may kill him."

"I have thought of it," Cowan said. And then he added, "I would like to get him out of this alive."

"It will be most difficult. If he makes the attempt to steal it—always admitting the treasure does exist— he will be killed. The General, my brother-in-law, has small liking for bandits. He is a just man, but stern."

Ben Cowan glanced at the Captain. Recalde had no business even being out of bed. It was exactly a week since they had arrived in Hermosillo, and this was the first time Recalde had been out. Even now he walked slowly, and with a cane.

Day after day and night after night Ben Cowan had searched the town, but he had found no sign of Catlow or any of his men, nor of Miller.

Where was the treasure? Where would the attempt

be made? A dozen men against an army . . . Surprise would be needed, and time . . . rarely could they be found together.

All the while, Ben Cowan had the uneasy feeling that he himself was being watched, and he thought back to the night someone had taken a shot at him in Tucson—had it been Miller? It might have been Rio Bray, or Old Man Merridew . . . except that the Old Man would not have missed.

His mind reverted to the problem of the theft. Surprise, of course; but time . . . time to get away with a treasure that could not be easily carried. Gold and silver are heavy, easily noticed, and sure to cause comment. It is easy, perhaps, to imagine gaining possession of a treasure worth millions, but it is something quite different when one actually has to move it.

When Ben Cowan had seen Recalde safely home, he strolled up the street to a cantina he had chosen to frequent, and pondered the problem over a bottle of cold beer.

How could the bandits get away? Burros or mules would be needed, and an escape route that was foolproof. Of course there was no such thing, but Bijah Catlow would have a plan. Impulsive he might be, but he was cunning as a wolf when cunning was needed.

Ben glanced around the room. It was almost deserted, for the siesta hour was near. Soon even these few would be gone. Catlow might choose to make his strike at such a time, and it was a thought to be remembered. If he could move when most of the town, even the soldiers, were napping, he might have a chance, and it was just the sort of idea to intrigue him.

Despite the insistence of Recalde, Ben Cowan was living at the Hotel Arcadia. Recalde had relatives in the town, and it was with them that he was living and recuperating from his wounds; but Ben Cowan wanted to be in the midst of things where he could see and hear what was going on, and consider his problems without paying attention to the courtesies of a private home.

The last Mexican had now left the cantina, and the proprietor glanced hopefully at Cowan, obviously wishing he would go. Ben finished his beer, decided against suggesting that he be allowed to remain and drink another bottle, and strolled out into the sunlight.

Hermosillo, with a population of less than fifteen thousand, was a pleasant little city on the banks of the Rio Sonora, lying among orange groves and gardens. Outside the town the valley was dotted with grain fields, and all was green and lovely. Now the streets were deserted, and Cowan missed the slender, graceful girls of Sonora, noted for its beautiful women.

He loitered under the shade of the huge old trees in the Plaza, and deep within their shade he must have been invisible to the man who stepped suddenly from a narrow wooden door in a side street off the Plaza.

As the man emerged, he took a swift glance around him, then hurried up the street. His confidence that at this hour he would be unobserved made him miss seeing Ben Cowan standing under the tree only fifty yards away.

The man was Bob Keleher, who had been with
Catlow on the trail drive, and who had been with him
at the campfire when Catlow killed Mercer.

To attempt to follow Keleher in the empty streets
would only betray Cowan's presence in Hermosillo,
of which they might not be aware, and to make the
man wary of exposing the hiding place chosen by
Catlow.

At the building Keleher had left, the shutters were
up and the door closed, but Ben Cowan, who had
spent his week getting acquainted with Hermosillo,
remembered the place as a leather-worker's shop. The
man dealt, as Moss Burton did, in fancy bridles, saddles, hand-tooled boots, and such things, doing his
work on the premises in full view of the passersby, for
the shop's front was open when business was being
carried on.

In one back corner there was a curtain of bridle
reins hanging down from the thick cluster of bridles
hung from hooks on the wall, near the ceiling. Those
bridle reins made a perfect screen for whatever might
lie behind. In the other corner there was a door leading to the living premises. But now the shutters were
up, and aside from the door to the street, the shop
front presented a blank wall to the eye.

Was Keleher only visiting in that house? Seeing a
girl, perhaps? Or was this the hideout of the gang, or
some of its members?

Leaving the shade of his tree, Ben walked slowly to
the next street. He glanced along it and saw that except for a large carriage gate there was only a blank
wall. Walking up the street, he paused opposite the

carriage gate and peered through the crack where the two doors of the gate met. He looked into a paved patio where an old wooden-wheeled cart stood, its tongue resting on the ground. The building just beside the gate was obviously, judging by the smell, a stable. He could see a part of the rear of the house where the leather-worker lived, but it was only a blank wall with one second-story window that was tightly shuttered.

Walking farther on, Cowan satisfied himself that the place had only two entrances, one at the front, and the other through the carriage gate at the back.

He returned to the Plaza and sat down on a bench and smoked a cigar while he considered the situation. From where he sat he could look up the street where the shop was situated, and after a moment he turned his attention to the building across the street from it.

On the second story of that building there were windows from which the leather shop might be observed. He considered briefly the idea of renting a room there, if one was available, and then decided against it. Unless there was a back entrance, his own coming and going could be too easily observed— anyway, he was not yet sure he had discovered anything of importance.

The siesta hour was almost past when Rio Bray came into the street and entered the door by which Keleher had left. Presently people began to appear on the street . . . after a little, shutters were taken down and life resumed its normal movement. Ben Cowan lighted another cigar and loafed in the shade, idly examining a newspaper.

The shutters of the leather shop came down and business, such as it was, resumed. From where he sat Ben could see part of the shop's interior, but nobody else came or left whom he recognized.

He started to fold his newspaper, preparatory to leaving, when someone paused near him. He saw the polished boots, the obviously tailored uniform trousers, and looked up into the face of General Juan Bautista Armijo.

"She is lovely," the General commented, "is she not?"

For a moment Ben Cowan did not realize what he meant, and then he saw the girl.

She was standing, poised and assured, on the street corner near the leather shop. Where she had come from he did not know, but he could see that she was, indeed, very striking-looking.

"I expect the General has seen her closer than this; but yes, I think she is pretty." Cowan got up, and Armijo turned to smile at him.

"You are still with us, señor. We are honored. Have you located your man?"

"No, not yet."

"You still believe he is here?"

"Perhaps not here, but certainly not far away."

Armijo dropped a cigarette into the dust and rubbed it out. "There will be a ball at my regimental headquarters this evening. I have asked the Captain to bring you, señor."

When he was gone, Ben Cowan looked thoughtfully after him. Had his sudden appearance here been an accident? Or was the General having him watched?

Did General Armijo, perhaps, know of what was going on at the leather shop?

There was room enough in that stable for a dozen horses to be hidden.

The girl on the corner had turned suddenly and was coming toward him.

# CHAPTER 14

I N THE SHADOWED coolness of the living quarters behind the leather shop, Bijah Catlow made his final plans. The door that led to the cellar where he and his men waited opened from behind the curtain of bridles, as Ben Cowan had half suspected.

There was a hallway of stone . . . the remainder of the house was of adobe, and of later construction. A stone stairway went down into the vast, ancient cellar. Here there were no windows, for the ceiling of the cellar was six feet below ground level, and as a matter of fact, its existence was unknown to the people of Hermosillo.

The builder of the adobe, itself one of the earliest buildings in the town, had utilized what remained of the ruin on this site. It was only after the house was built, when making excavations for repairs, that he had found the vast underground room. Being a wise man, and a discreet one, he had mentioned the find to no one, and he and his sons had finished the work by themselves.

The origin of the ruin was a mystery. This might have been the site of some planned mission, where construction had ceased because of Apache attacks . . . records of many such had vanished from the country with the Jesuits. Or it might have been still older . . . perhaps an Indian ruin reaching back in time even before the Aztecs.

The owner of the leather shop had himself been a bandit, as his father had been before him, and from time to time, through revolution and change, they had found use for the ancient cellar.

There was an exit, a secret way that opened into the stables . . . this had been built by the present owner's grandfather on the principle that not even a rat trusts himself to one hole only. In the planning of the present robbery, Pesquiera, the owner of the leather shop, had shared his secret with Bijah Catlow. But now they were of two minds. Pesquiera wanted the gold brought into his cellar and held there until the chase had died down. Bijah Catlow wanted it spirited out of the country quickly. As a matter of fact, Bijah did not entirely trust his Mexican partner, nor his nephew, the deserter who had come to him in Tucson.

Pesquiera had known of the treasure for years, but had known only approximately where it was hidden; and Lerdo was shrewd enough to see that living nearby to guard it were loyal members of a family distantly related to his own. There had been no chance until now, when the treasure would be moved, to lay hands upon it.

Bijah had an idea that, once that treasure was hidden in the secret cellar, some accident would happen to destroy his men and himself, or a trap would be laid for them. He preferred to trust himself to the open desert and the risks of flight, no matter how great they might be.

He sat alone now at a table, and stared at the glass

of beer before him, but he was not thinking of the beer. He was thinking of what lay before him.

In a corner, some thirty feet away, several of the men played at cards. In a nearby room, others were asleep. He had been careful to allow none of them to be seen around town, and the men he had on watch at a particular point changed watches only during the time of siesta.

Two things disturbed him. One of these was what he had learned of the character of General Armijo. He was no lackadaisical officeholder, but a competent and experienced soldier and a man of the desert. He had behind him twenty years of war in the field. He had fought in revolutions in his own country, against the French, and against the Apaches. Armijo had only recently been transferred to Sonora, but he knew the country. Bijah Catlow had not reckoned on Armijo.

The other factor that worried him was the whereabouts of Ben Cowan. Bijah had neither seen nor heard of him since that night in Tucson, but he was all the more worried because of that.

He rubbed the stubble on his broad jaw and swore softly. The other men were restless, and he did not blame them, sitting for days in a dark cellar, unable to show their faces on the street of a town known for its beautiful women. And when they did emerge it would only be to make a quick strike and escape.

For a moment he stared gloomily about the room. Catlow was nothing if not a perceptive man, and it came to him suddenly that he had taken a direction that might keep him among such associates, and in such surroundings for the remainder of his years. He might spend his life hiding in abandoned ranch houses, cheap hotel rooms, on the dodge, never sure from one minute to the next when the law might come up to him. He glanced at the table across the room . . . there was only one man in the lot whom he really liked—Old Man Merridew.

He gulped a swallow of beer and thought again of the two millions . . . with his share of that, a man could live anywhere, do just about anything.

Yet the gloomy thoughts remained with him, brought on in part by the surroundings, the dark and ancient cellar, the foul air, and by the boredom of waiting.

Because he did not trust Pesquiera, he had stalled on making a decision as to where the treasure would be taken. The risks of trying to get it into the cellar were great . . . if the pack train was seen in the street, that would be an end to it. The plan now called for a midnight strike, for they had learned when the treasure was to reach the town, but Catlow had worked out an alternative plan of which he had said nothing to anyone.

The close confinement was having its effect upon him, too. Even less than the others was he fitted to put up with the restricted quarters, for Bijah Catlow was a man who liked people. He liked gaiety and friendliness, he liked bright lights and music, cheerful talk, and the casual argument and rawhiding that went with any cattle drive or roundup. Yet he must wait in hiding now. He settled down to considering his plans, but his mind kept drifting off at a tangent.

Christina had promised to buy a box of cigars for him, and she should be coming back soon. He got up and wandered over to the poker game, watched gloomily for a few minutes, and then went to the steps.

Bill Joiner looked after him and spoke irritably. "We don't get a chance to move one step out of here, but he goes whenever he's of a mind to."

Rio Bray, too, had been staring after Catlow, but he merely shrugged. "Somebody has to keep in touch, and this is his strike. He laid it out, he brought us in."

Joiner was a border outlaw; some said he had been a scalp hunter. He was a tall, thin man with a mean expression that never left his eyes, even when he smiled, which was rarely enough. Jealousy was a major part of his make-up—that, and distrust.

Catlow had accepted him reluctantly, and he had done so because he was a dead shot with any sort of weapon, could ride all day and all night, and was a man of known courage.

Catlow went up the steps and, avoiding the narrow passage that led to the shop, opened a concealed door and emerged into the living quarters of the family.

Christina was in the kitchen, putting dishes on a tray. She was slender for a Mexican girl, as the Sonora women are apt to be, and her carriage and figure were excellent. He glanced at her with admiration, and she gave him a sidelong glance from her dark, almost almond-shaped eyes.

"You should not be here. My father does not like it."

"Then I wouldn't see you," he said, "and I'd risk trouble with your pa any time for that." He watched her as she put the large bowl of frijoles on the tray, with the tortillas and some large slabs of roast pork.

"You get my cigars?"

"*Si*"—she indicated the box on a side table—"I get them." She paused, then added, "I saw an Americano . . . a gringo in the Plaza."

Catlow was watching the movements of her body as she worked about the room, and scarcely heard her.

"He was a stranger," she added.

"Who was?"

"The gringo. He looked at me." She glanced at Catlow to see the effect of her words.

"Be a damn' fool if he didn't. A gringo, you say? Maybe a tall man? A quiet-lookin' man? Only smiles with his eyes?"

She shrugged. "He is ver' handsome, this *hombre*. He wears a black suit and talks with the General Armijo. I heard the General invite him to the ball."

"Ball?"

"Oh, *si!* Everybody talk about it. I think everybody will be there . . . all the officers, the—how you say it?—the important ones . . . the reech ones."

Catlow considered. According to his information, the treasure was due to arrive in Hermosillo tomorrow. At this moment it was guarded by several hundred soldiers, and any attempt to seize it would be suicidal. He had planned his move to take place at midnight following the arrival in Hermosillo, when the guard was going off duty, eager to get to bed and letting down after the long march and the necessity for keeping watch.

They would be tired and sleepy, and thinking of anything but the treasure they had guarded. It worried him that Armijo was now in charge, for the officer scheduled to be in command had been easygoing and anything but efficient.

Suppose, however, that the treasure train arrived *tonight?*

He had men watching for the train, and he knew about how fast such a pack train could move; but suppose there was added reason to reach Hermosillo tonight?

He glanced at Christina and said, "Do you know the officer in charge of the train?"

"Of course. There are three."

"Old men?"

"*Old?* Very young! And very handsome, too, they are." She gestured toward the tray. "Do you wish to take this? I cannot."

"Sure." He picked up the tray, and then said, "You know about such things—are any of those men in love?"

She laughed. "Mexican men are always in love. When they are not in love with a particular girl they are in love with love. Why not? It is the way for a man to be."

"I won't argue with you. But one of these officers, one of them who is really excited about a girl . . . Maybe she has not shown him much favor— or maybe she has, and he wants to get back to her in a hurry."

"Rafael Vargas," she said, tossing her head, "he can think of no one but Señorita Calderon . . . and she—he does not know what she thinks."

Catlow grinned. "Honey," he said, "you get me a

box of the finest stationery you can find! Do you hear?" He placed several silver pesos on the table. "You do that, and I'll—"

The door opened suddenly, and Pesquiera stood there, his features dark with anger.

# CHAPTER 15

PESQUIERA'S RIGHT HAND gripped a pistol. "You!" he said to Bijah. "Get out of here! You are not to speak to my daughter, do you understand?"

Catlow smiled. "This is business," he said, "something only she can do. I need some writing paper, the kind a woman would buy, and there was no time to waste. She must go for it now."

Pesquiera's gun did not waver. "Why is this? What do you plan?"

"It is a change in plans if it works, and I think it will work. The robbery tonight instead of tomorrow night."

Slowly the gun lowered. "Tonight?" Pesquiera said stupidly. "But it will not arrive tonight! And there are many soldiers!"

Catlow turned to Christina. "Get that stationery, will you? Get it now!"

When she was gone, Catlow sat down. "I'm sorry you got riled," he said, "but we have to move fast." Briefly, he explained about the man he believed might be Ben Cowan, and his meeting with Armijo. "If that young captain gets this note," he said, "he will come a-running. He will want to meet her at the dance, and the dance is tonight. He'll run the legs off those mules gettin' here . . . and there'll be no guard waitin' to take over."

Pesquiera's expression changed. "You are right, and I am a fool."

"Look"—Catlow leaned toward him confidentially— "not only will there be no guard, but Vargas will be hurryin' to get ready for that dance. He'll be late, anyway . . . everything will be in a mess."

———

BEN COWAN RETURNED to his room in the Arcadia to change his clothes for the ball. He was combing his hair in front of the mirror, thinking about the evening ahead of him. Only once before had he been to such a ball as he expected this to be, and that had been at the Governor's mansion in Austin.

He sat down on the bed and polished his boots as best he could, then swung his cartridge belt around his waist and drew it several notches tighter than he usually wore it, so it would ride higher.

As he was holstering his six-gun Recalde entered. "You are not carrying a gun *tonight?*" he said, amused. "At the General's ball there will scarcely be use for it."

"I wouldn't feel at home without it. And a man never knows what'll happen."

Recalde sat down, easing his wounded leg out before him. He leaned his cane against the side of the chair. "After all, *amigo,* the pack train does not even arrive until tomorrow."

Ben Cowan slid into his black coat and Recalde watched him, smiling. "I can see you will make hearts flutter tonight," the Mexican said. "You have no idea how much interest you have created in Hermosillo.

After all, it is a small town, and we have few strangers here—fewer still who are friends of the General."

"Of yours, you mean."

"Of the General's also. You would be surprised, but he has spoken of you several times. He even asked me to speak to you about joining him in the army. You would be an officer, and the General is close to the President. It might mean a very quick success for you."

"I'm not cut out for a soldier," Cowan replied. "I'm too damned independent. I like to go my own way, figure things out for myself. I think the General has plenty of savvy, and I'd not mind serving with *him* . . . but it might be I'd be serving with some armchair soldier. No, I'm better off as I am."

"He will regret your decision." Recalde used his cane to rise. "Let us go."

A carriage awaited them. Ben Cowan felt odd, riding in the open carriage, but he saw several like it, all polished and bright, hurrying toward the huge old building where the ball was to be held. It was not often such a thing happened in a provincial town like Hermosillo, and the señoritas were in from all the haciendas for miles around.

As their carriage took its turn around the Plaza, which all the carriages seemed to be doing, Ben Cowan glanced up the dark street where the leather shop stood. All was dark and still.

The night was cool after the heat of the day, and it was pleasant riding about the Plaza behind the driver who sat on a high seat in front of them. People bowed and smiled, speaking to Recalde, and glancing curiously at him.

Young Captain Recalde was not only an unusually handsome man, but he had wealth and tradition behind him. Ben Cowan could guess that not a few of those at the ball tonight were going to be looking hopefully in his direction. For young men of family, from the capital, rarely had occasion to visit Hermosillo.

"Vargas will not like to miss this," Recalde commented; "he fancies himself in love. I happen to know he has been writing notes and smuggling them secretly to Rosita Calderon—only it is the worst-kept secret in town."

Ben Cowan smiled in the darkness. It was much the same on both sides of the border. A man would make an unholy fool of himself over a pretty girl—but that was the privilege of any young man, and they all had to do it once or twice.

"He's the man in command?"

"Yes . . . and a good soldier, but impatient."

They drove at last to the ball, and Ben Cowan decided it was worth it. He had never seen so many really beautiful women . . . dark, flashing eyes that glanced at him from behind their fans . . . here and there a redhead or even a blonde among all those with dark hair.

Recalde was looking romantically pale from his recent wounds, and he was very smart in his uniform a-glitter with braid and decorations.

Ben sat down beside him and they talked as the people entered and moved about the room. Recalde kept up a running comment. "Now that one"—he indicated with an inclination of his head a tall young girl with large, melting dark eyes—"her father has more cattle on his ranch than there is in your whole state of New Mexico . . . right at this time, at least. But she is too—shall we say—intelligent. She has nothing to do on that ranch, so she reads . . . she thinks, also. It is dangerous in a woman."

Ben Cowan glanced at her again. She was not exactly beautiful, but she was very striking. Later, when he danced with her, she said, "You are the friend of Captain Recalde? He is handsome, your friend, but he believes every girl wishes to marry him." She laughed suddenly, with genuine amusement, and looked at Ben, her eyes smiling. "And you know? He is right. They all wish it."

"You too?"

"I scarcely know him, but I do not think he will want a wife like me." She gave Ben a direct, friendly glance that he liked. "I ride the range with my father, you know . . . sometimes without him. It is not considered the thing to do.

"And I read books. Most young men wish their wives to be beautiful, but complacent—and not too bright, I am afraid."

"I think Recalde should have a wife such as you," Ben said. "I know he wishes for a career in government, and an intelligent wife could help him."

"It is an American viewpoint."

He glanced at her, suddenly embarrassed. "You know, I did not get your name."

"I am Rosita Calderon."

He was startled. This was the girl with whom Captain Vargas was in love—or with whom he fancied himself in love. Suddenly, the thought of Vargas worried him. Did Vargas know about this ball? If so, he must be frustrated at not being present . . . surely, he would know that Rosita Calderon would be here.

By this time he would not be too many miles from Hermosillo. . . .

"Excuse me," he said suddenly, brusquely, "I must go."

He was almost running when he reached the head of the steps. Recalde called out to him, but he did not stop.

He plunged down the steps and out into the street. The long row of waiting carriages stood on the far side under the trees, and several of the drivers were together in a group, talking. They looked around at him, surprised at his sudden appearance. There was no one else in sight.

Swiftly, he ran to the corner and looked down the street toward the barracks and the courtyard. A sentry stood on guard at the entrance. Ben went toward him.

He spoke quickly in Spanish. "Have you seen the—"

He heard the light, quick step behind him and started to turn. Something crashed down hard across his skull and he slumped forward, fighting to keep on his feet. He fell against the side of the building and tried to turn, but another blow felled him into the street.

He smelled the dust . . . and there was blood, too. His blood.

A hand grasped his collar and he was dragged around the corner. Somebody was swearing.

A voice said: "Who is it?"

"That damn' marshal friend of Catlow's."

"To hell with him."

There was a momentary silence. Then someone said, "With Catlow, too."

Another silence, and then the first voice spoke again. "Everything in its time, my friend. But we understand each other, no?"

Ben heard, but he could not act. He could not even think. He had no will to act, to think, even to try to move. He simply lay still, and then after a while he was conscious of nothing at all . . . nothing.

---

DIEGO RECALDE STOOD up with an effort. After sitting, his leg became stiff, and it was difficult to handle himself with ease. His doctor had told him emphatically that he must not come out tonight, but Diego Recalde had already been planning which of his dress uniforms he would wear.

Now he glanced toward the door. Ben had left suddenly at least a half hour ago, and he had not come back. It was not like him to do such a thing.

Limping, Recalde crossed the room to Rosita Calderon. She turned to meet him, smiling a little. "You have waited a long time to speak to me, Diego," she said. "Are you still frightened of me?"

"Who is frightened?" She was lovely, he admitted, and there was a frankness about her that he liked. Came from riding around like a boy, or maybe from that American cousin she had—a cousin by marriage, at least. What was his name? Sackett, or something like that. Lived in New Mexico.

"What did you say to my friend? To Benito? He left here as if you had insulted him."

"Do women insult men? I think not until they know them better than I know him. No, he just left suddenly—and rudely."

"You said nothing to him?"

She frowned. "Nothing . . . unless he does not like my name. When we were introduced he did not hear it, I suppose, and he asked me what it was. I told him, and he ran away."

"I cannot ask you to dance," Recalde said then. "You see I was—"

"I know, and I am sorry."

He frowned, worrying over Ben Cowan's sudden departure.

"You told him your *name*, you say? That would scarcely have meant anything to him. Why, I mentioned you this evening, and he did not seem to have ever heard the name."

Still puzzled, he glanced across the room to where General Armijo was talking casually with a white-haired man, Don Francisco Vargas.

"*Vargas!*"

He wheeled suddenly, forgetting his leg, and fell flat upon his face as it gave way under him.

"*General!*" he shouted. "*The pack train!*"

# CHAPTER 16

BIJAH CATLOW'S NOTE, written by Christina and signed with the name of Rosita Calderon, reached Rafael Vargas as swiftly as a rider could take it, and Vargas reacted as Catlow had expected.

Excited at the prospect of seeing the girl who had seemed uninterested until now, and of dancing with her, Vargas had driven the pack train at a fast pace over trails where normally they would have plodded. Surely, General Armijo would be pleased to have him arrive sooner than expected.

Up and down the column Vargas rode, urging the muleteers to greater speed. Impatient at the slowness of the exhausted mules, he wished to ride on, leaving the train to follow, but he was wise enough to realize the General would not be pleased at that.

When finally they arrived in Hermosillo the streets were dark and silent. The soldiers, who had been kept alert for a time by their swift ride, now felt its effects, and weariness came over them; they thought of nothing but their barracks, a hot meal, and bed. Sagging in the saddle, half asleep, they rode into the courtyard, and Vargas swung from the saddle, turning to his second in command.

"Lieutenant," he said to Fernandes, "see to the unloading and storage of the cargo, then bring the keys to me. I want a guard posted at once, subject to removal only on orders from General Armijo."

He turned swiftly, and a man stepped from the darkness of a doorway. A gun in the hands of Rio Bray shocked him into his first realization that he had walked into a trap.

Rosita Calderon was forgotten; the distant strains of dance music seemed to come from another world. The courtyard was silent and dark, but he could see clearly enough to make out that his men were being disarmed and backed to the wall.

Everything moved swiftly. The mules were turned toward the gate, the disarmed soldiers marched to the guardhouse.

Captain Rafael Vargas was a brave man. He was also a sensible one—up to a point. With a shock of cold realization, he knew the note for what it was—a trick. Rosita Calderon had not changed, and he had been betrayed. Mexico was about to be robbed.

Somebody stepped up behind him and a hand unsnapped the flap of his holster. Vargas whipped around like a cat, knocking away the grasping hand, and drew his pistol.

A blow staggered him, and then a gun muzzle was thrust under his heart. Something exploded there, and Vargas turned, squeezing off a wild, futile shot that lost itself in the earth at his feet, and then he fell.

Bijah Catlow rushed up, the taste of anger bitter in his mouth. He stared down at the dead man. It was bad—he had hoped to kill no one.

"Get going!" he said to Bray. "There's no time!"

Catlow had no idea that riding the saddle of a

captured horse was the one man he did not want anywhere around . . . Ben Cowan.

Ben Cowan was unconscious. He had fought against the wave of darkness creeping over him, but had lost the fight. Tied now in the saddle, his body bobbed with the movement of the horse. Pesquiera had wanted to knife him, but Rio Bray had ruled against it. "You don't know Catlow," he said. "I'd never want to be the man who killed Ben Cowan."

As the men moved up the dark street, Pesquiera rode in beside Catlow. "The cellar!" he said, sharply.

"No."

"They will never find us there!"

"If they don't find us on the trails they will go through this town like it has never been gone through before. They would find us—and the gold."

But Catlow was not altogether sure of that. He was sure, though, that once that gold got into Pesquiera's secret cellar, it would never get out. He was equally sure that the Mexican had no intention for it ever to get away from Hermosillo.

Nor for them to get away, for that matter. A little poison in their food—and they would have nowhere else to get food—and it would be an end to them. That ancient cellar could conceal bodies as well as gold, as no doubt it had.

Pesquiera gripped his gun butt. "It must be the cellar," he declared, "or—"

Catlow smiled, and Pesquiera did not like what he saw in that smile. "You go ahead, *amigo*," Catlow said. "You draw that gun."

Pesquiera hesitated, and the moment was past.

"You may be right," he said; "but your friend—it would be wise to leave him here, no?"

It was the first that Bijah Catlow had known of Cowan's presence. There was no more time to be wasted, and Bijah did not want Ben Cowan along. "All right," he said, "leave him here."

———

By THE TIME Recalde had explained to General Armijo what he believed was happening, the pack train was leaving the outskirts of Hermosillo.

The first wild rush of cavalry went out the trail toward the border, assuming that Catlow, being an American, would lead his men that way. And they found nothing. Other detachments scattered in several directions, all of them wrong.

Bijah Catlow, with characteristic cunning, had led his pack train down back streets, where they made no sound in the soft dust. Turning from a trail, he took them through an orchard, then opened the gate on the irrigation ditch just enough so it might appear to be an accident but would successfully flood the orchard, wiping out all tracks.

Through country lanes, past orchards and wheatfields, Catlow led his mule train, the animals staggering from weariness. Twice he paused to open corral gates and allow animals to get out that would destroy the trail they had left. Finally, with the mules more dead than alive, he herded them into a pole corral on the edge of a small arroyo. Nearby was a dam. The ranch itself was deserted, and apparently had been for some time.

In another, larger corral, among the trees on the

far side of a low butte, fresh mules awaited him. Swiftly exchanging packsaddles and loads, Catlow led the train off toward the northwest. He had told no one his plans, nor did he intend to.

On the skyline, more than a dozen miles away toward the northwest, was the Cerro Cuevas, a low mountain range that stood out above the comparatively level plain. The trail toward it was a long-unused one. When they came close to the mountains, a Mexican was waiting by the trail to guide them into the caves.

It was midday when they unsaddled inside the caves. Old Man Merridew climbed up among the rocks and settled down to watch. The rest ate, slept, and waited for Catlow to tell them what he planned. But Catlow said nothing.

He had two million dollars in gold and silver and, aside from the Old Man, there was not a one among them he could trust.

If he was unlucky, the mules would be found at the abandoned ranch before the day was out. If he was lucky, they might remain there for several days before some searcher happened upon them. The route he was taking was the least likely of any that could be found. Just as he had done when slipping into Mexico, now in slipping out he intended to use the least-known route and the least-known water holes. But if the men with him had any idea of what they faced he would have mutiny on his hands.

It was a hot, still day. After a while the Tarahumara went up to relieve the Old Man.

Merridew came and squatted near Catlow. "Nothin'

stirrin'," he commented. "Seemed a sight of dust over east, but that might have been anything."

"How'd Cowan happen to stumble on us?" Catlow asked.

The Old Man shrugged. "Durned if I know. Pesky was takin' over the sentry's job so's everythin' would look all right. He says Cowan came up there in a rush and started to ask a question. Rio Bray slugged him."

"Cowan's too smart."

"Well," Merridew replied dryly, "if they got him locked in that there cellar, he'll keep for a time. Lucky if he ever gets out, if that Christina takes after her pa."

Catlow looked from the mouth of the cave toward the north. "Didn't you tell me you'd been down to the Rio Concepcion one time?"

Merridew shot him a startled glance. "Look here, you ain't figurin' on *that* route, are you? There's no water—or so damn' little it don't matter."

"All the more reason. They won't be lookin' for us there, Old Man. Look"—squatting, he drew a rough diagram in the sand—"there's the border . . . over here is the Gulf of California. The main trail from Hermosillo to Tucson is yonder. Here's where we are. And here"—he indicated a spot on the sand—"is Pozo Arivaipa—'*pozo*' meaning well."

The Old Man looked up. "How far is it between here and that *pozo* you speak of?"

Catlow lowered his voice to a whisper. "Maybe sixty miles—as the crow flies."

"*Sixty miles?* Without water? With mules?"

Catlow lifted a hand. "See here? Right there is the Rio Bacoachi. It's about sixteen miles out. Now, it ain't a reg'lar river. In fact, it flows only part of the time—we might have to dig for water there. But we've had a wet spring . . . I think it's a good chance."

"You goin' to tell them?"

"No—not until I have to."

Merridew squinted his eyes at the desert. "You're shapin' for trouble, Bijah. I tell you, this lot won't stand for it—not Pesky, nor Rio either, for that matter."

"Rio's been with me as long as you have."

"There's a difference. I'm a *segundo*. I never aimed or figured to be owner or foreman. Rio, he figures he's smarter than you. He goes along, but it chafes him. It really chafes him. Here lately it's been worse, so don't you put faith in Rio Bray."

"What about the others?"

"I'd say Keleher—you can count on him. And the Injun. That Injun likes you, and I don't think he cottons to any of the rest of us. If trouble breaks, it might split fifty-fifty, and it might not break so good for us."

Catlow nodded. "That's about the way I figured, Old Man; but we need them, and once we get far enough into that godforsaken desert, they're going to need me—like it or not."

When the sun went down they moved out, Bijah leading off. He started at a good clip deliberately, to keep them so busy there was no time to ask questions. He pulled his hat low over his eyes and looked north into the desert. He knew what he was going into, and what was likely to happen before he got out—if he ever did.

The last man off the mountain reported no sign

of pursuit, and from where he had been watching he could see for miles, with the setting sun making the land bright.

On top of a low rise, Catlow drew up to let the mule train bunch a little and to look over the country. Old Man Merridew had not asked the question Bijah had been fearing; and fortunately, the Tarahumara did not talk. The desert, the lack of water, and the heat . . . they were bad enough, but the country into which they were riding was the land of the Seri Indians.

Usually, the Seris held to the coast except when raiding, or to their stronghold on Tiburon Island, in the Gulf of California. Fierce as the Apaches— Catlow had heard rumors they were cannibals—they had devastated large areas of country, and he was leading the mule train right into the region where they traveled to and from their raids.

But he was gambling on avoiding them, or even defeating them; and as for water, there had been heavy spring rains. Though now it was nearly July, from late July through August and September there were occasional heavy rains in Sonora—rains that fell suddenly upon relatively small areas, then vanished to leave it hotter than before. But for a time they left water in the water holes.

Anyway, there was no other way to get out of Mexico with two million dollars in gold and silver.

Again they pushed on steadily through the warm night.

Two hours passed before the inevitable question was asked, and it was Rio who asked it. "Is there plenty of water where we're going to camp?"

"We're not going to camp. Not until nearly morning, at least."

"Hell, Bijah, everybody's about done in."

"By now," Catlow replied shortly, "Armijo has cavalry scouring the country. Maybe he's found the mules we left behind, maybe not. An' you know how far we've got to go? Maybe two hundred miles."

"We got to rest," Rio said stubbornly.

"You'll rest," Catlow replied, "when we get where we're goin'—not before."

It was rough, broken country. They rode down into arroyos, crossed long stretches of hard-topped mesa, waded through ankle-deep sand. Day was just breaking when they looked down upon a maze of arroyos, the broken watercourses of the Bacoachi . . . and there was no water in sight.

"Where's the water?" Rio demanded. "I thought there was water."

"Get the shovels," Catlow said.

"*Shovels?*" Rio swore. "I'll be damned if I'll—"

"Give me one of them," Keleher said quietly. "Come on, Old Man. You could always find water."

They found it two feet beneath the surface, and it welled up in quantity wherever they dug. The mules watered; Rio Bray was silent and sullen.

"Fill your canteens and all the kegs," Catlow told them. "It will be forty, fifty miles to the next water."

Nobody said a word—they simply stared at him. Bob Keleher gathered up the shovels and lashed them in place on the pack mules. Now he knew why Bijah had been insistent on loading four mules with two water kegs each.

Loafing and resting in the shadows of the river

bank, Catlow thought ahead. This was going to be the toughest job he'd ever tackled . . . and he figured that by now they had found his trail—or the mules, at least.

They would be coming after him, but he was not worried about their catching him—not that, so much as their heading him off. Would they think of that? Would they leave his trail, gambling on riding ahead along trails where there was plenty of water and where they could travel much faster than he, and then heading him off before he could reach the border?

Or would they think that perhaps he had a boat waiting somewhere along the Gulf Coast, ready to pick him up and carry him out of their reach?

Catlow tasted the brackish water and looked at the mules. There were no better mules in the country, and he had prepared them for this. Despite the fast pace, they were in good shape.

Some miles away to the west lay a dark blue range of mountains. There were low hills between, but it was the mountains that were important—more important at that moment than Bijah Catlow knew.

High on a serrated ridge a lone Seri huddled against a pinnacle of rock and looked out toward the east. His sharp eyes picked out a faint thread of smoke . . . a beckoning finger lifting a mute question toward the sky.

The Seri ground some seed between his broken molars, and squinted into the distance. Smoke meant men, men meant horses, and horses were meat. . . . He was hungry for meat.

The hard black eyes watched that finger of smoke and considered. It might be the Army; but the Army rarely came into this land, and then only after some raid by the Seris into settled land—and there had been no such raid.

Rising, he looked eastward once more; then he turned and began to slide down off the rocks. He was several miles from his camp, but he was in no hurry. He knew the country that lay before those marching men.

It would not be hard tomorrow, but the next day it would be easier . . . much easier.

# CHAPTER 17

BEN COWAN'S FIRST conscious awareness was of a musty odor. He lay for what seemed a long time and could sense only that, and a dull throbbing in his skull. Then he opened his eyes, or he thought he opened them—but it remained dark. He could hear nothing—no sound, no sense of movement anywhere.

He was lying sprawled on a stone floor. . . . And then full awareness returned, and with it full realization. He had rushed from the ballroom to the barrack courtyard, and he had started to ask a question of the sentry. It was at that moment that he had been struck down from behind.

Now he got his palms flat on the floor and pushed himself to a sitting position. His hand went to his holster. His gun was gone.

Feeling for the .44 derringer he habitually carried in his waistband, he found that was gone, too. Of course it would be. Catlow knew of that gun.

Ben stared into the darkness around him. He was in absolute blackness. He put out a hand, but touched nothing. On hands and knees he began to crawl, and brought up against something—a chair leg. He felt the chair and stood up, holding to the back. His head swam, and he clung shakily to the chair back until the confusion in his skull settled down.

There was no smallest ray of light to allow him to see anything. He must be in some sort of an underground place—a dungeon perhaps.

He felt in his pockets for matches and found none . . . they had been taken from him, too.

If there was a chair, then people sometimes sat here, hence there might be a table. Carefully, he felt around him, but found nothing. Finally, using the chair, he moved about, keeping it with him. If necessary it could be a weapon, or he might break off a chair leg.

Suddenly he paused. He had a faint but distinct impression of heat. Keeping one hand on the chair, he knelt and slowly crawled around it. He was almost all the way around the chair when he felt the heat quite distinctly on his cheek. Moving in that direction, he discovered a hearth and a fireplace.

It was cool down here, but not cool enough to need a fire. Someone must have been cooking, or perhaps making coffee, and there was still warmth there. Feeling around the edge of the fireplace, he found the end of an unburned stick, and he picked it up carefully. Then he moved his hand until he located the place of greatest warmth. Here he poked at the coals with the stick, uncovering some that glowed faintly red. He placed the stick upon them and blew, ever so gently. There was a smell of smoke, but nothing more.

Pulling out his shirttail, he tore a small piece from it and edged it against the coals. There was more smoke, and then a little flame. He saw the ends of more sticks and pushed them into the fire. The flames leaped up, and then he saw a coffeepot on the hearth and several cups at the edge. He rinsed a cup with a little coffee, then filled it and drank.

The coffee was very strong, but it was hot, and after a few gulps he felt better. He found more pieces of wood for fuel and added them to the fire. Then he stood up and looked around.

As well as he could tell, he was in a large, low-roofed room with stone walls and ceiling. No doors were visible, and no windows. There was a table, and several more chairs. On the floor were stubs of cigarettes and cigars, quite a lot of them.

There were also some empty beer bottles. He picked up one of these, hefted it, and placed it close at hand in the shadow. Then he placed others at various points about the room.

In so doing he found the door, but the latch would not give and the door itself was flat with the wall. It was strongly made of heavy oak planks, and he thought it must be reinforced on the other side with iron bars.

Carefully, he paced the room, studying the walls, the ceiling, the floor. He found nothing that offered any chance of escape.

And yet . . . there was something. . . .

The room was musty, as a place long closed might be, or one poorly ventilated. But he had smelled something else, some distance from the fire.

The room was all of sixty feet long and more than half that in width, and he tried pacing back and forth again, pausing at intervals. He had moved several feet before he again detected the faint odor. He hesitated there, then walked slowly back, testing the air.

Nothing. . . .

Or . . . ? He waited, breathing naturally, and suddenly it came to him. The faintest of odors, and yet it was definitely there. What he smelled was a stable—a horse stable.

He went back to the fire and added fuel from a pile nearby, and then, taking a blazing brand, he walked back and held it up toward the ceiling, which was only two feet or so above his head. There, beyond any doubt, was a trapdoor.

Returning his brand to the fire, he was about to make an attempt on the door when he heard the rattle of a bar being removed, and then the outer door opened. Standing in the door, holding a candle in one hand and a pistol in the other, was the girl he had seen from the park when he was talking to the General.

There was no mistaking the menace of the pistol.

"You don't need that," he said quietly. "I am not given to attacking women."

"Try it, if you like," she replied carelessly. "Shooting you might settle a lot of problems."

"The General was very attracted to you. If I were you, I'd develop his acquaintance."

The black eyes stared into his disdainfully. With a gesture, she indicated the doorway. "There is food . . . get it."

He looked at the food, which was on a tray standing just outside the door. It was an invitation to escape, and yet . . . he had a sudden realization that she wanted an excuse to kill him. But why?

"I am not hungry."

An odd light seemed to blaze in her eyes, but it

might have been his imagination—or some effect of the candlelight.

He looked at her curiously. "You are lovely," he said, "just the sort Bijah might prefer."

"And not you?"

"No . . . not me." He was watching her closely. Now he turned his back on the door and walked over to the fire. "Will you have some coffee? It's strong, but good."

"No."

She reminded him of a puma or a leopard. She moved in the same way, and there was an odd sense of expectancy about her, as if she awaited some signal from within herself that would tell her it was time to kill.

"Do you think you will ever see Bijah again? Women like Bijah," he added. "I envy him his way with them . . . he never seems to be anything but at ease, sure of himself."

"And you are not?"

"With women? Never." He added a stick to the fire. "I guess I never saw enough of them for the new to wear off. Or maybe I am simply sort of green."

The pistol muzzle was a black mouth that watched him. She would be a good shot, he decided; instinct and hatred would point that pistol, and nothing was more deadly.

It was women like this one who made fools of the schools of marksmanship. The way to fire a pistol was to draw and point as one pointed a finger. In many cases, the more time taken, the more apt one was to miss. How many times had he known of women, and sometimes men, who had never fired a gun before but who picked one up and scored with the first shot? But this was only in anger or fear. In practice on a target range they probably could hit nothing.

"Is he your father? The man who owns the leather shop?"

"He was my mother's husband, not my father." Her eyes seemed to flicker. "She was too weak for him, too soft."

"And you?"

She laughed suddenly. "I am too hard for him. He listens to Bijah, and would let you live. I shall not. I shall kill you."

She turned suddenly and went up the steps, but she turned at the door and pushed the tray with her foot. It slid to the top step, spilling some beans in the process. She closed the door abruptly, and he heard the bar fall in place.

He glanced toward the tray, then hesitated, and after a while took only the tortillas from it. If she planned to poison him it would be in the more highly seasoned food . . . he hoped.

Sitting by the fire, he ate the tortillas and drank more coffee. Then he took the sturdiest chair—all of them were solidly built—and carried it over under the trapdoor. Standing on the chair, he tried pushing up on the door. But it did not give.

He braced himself well and pushed upward again, with all his strength. He thought he detected just the faintest give. He tried again. Something was piled on top of the door, he decided, something heavy.

Then he brought the table over under the door and got up on it. Being closer to the door now, he could exert more pressure. He tried again, and this time the give was more decided.

He got down then and put the chair on top of the table, and by getting up on the chair he could put his back and shoulder against the door. He heaved, and something up there moved, and the door opened several inches on one side. He heaved again, something rolled off the door, and the door was freed. He pushed it open.

Grain sacks . . . grain sacks filled probably with corn had been placed over the door to conceal it. Ben straightened up, put his hands on the granary floor, and lifted himself up.

At the moment his heels cleared the opening he heard the rattle of the bar, a muffled cry, and then a shot. Something struck his boot heel and he jerked back from the door and slammed it in place. A swift heave put a grain sack on top of it.

He looked about him quickly. There were horses in the barn, and he was going to need a horse.

How she got there so fast, he never knew, but suddenly, as he hesitated over whether to take a horse or just to go without one, the girl appeared.

Christina's face was white, her eyes deep black, and her breast was heaving with emotion and the running she had done. She lifted the pistol and he felt the heat of its blast as he dove, hitting her with his shoulder and knocking her backwards into the hay.

She fought like a wildcat, writhing away from him, clubbing at him with the gun barrel, and trying to bring the muzzle down on him.

He grasped the gun around the action, gripping the cylinder and forcing her hand back. She tried to sink her teeth into his hand, but he wrenched the gun free and threw it from them.

Twisting, she clawed at his eyes with both hands, raking his face with her nails. He caught her wrists and pinned them down. He had never hit a woman, and did not want to do it now, but this was no ordinary woman; she was an animal, half cat, half devil.

Between gasps he said, "I do not want to hit you!"

She spat in his face.

Her blouse was torn, and quickly he averted his eyes. She laughed at him. "Coward!" she sneered.

He picked her up bodily and threw her down in the hay, then ducked out of the door. The outer gate to the street was locked, so he jumped, caught at the top, and pulled himself up. A bullet clipped the wood near his hand, and he heard the bellow of the pistol. He threw himself over and fell into the street.

A big vaquero was adjusting the stirrup on his saddle. He glanced at the torn shirt, the bloody scratches on Ben's face, and he laughed. "Ah, señor! I have heard of this one! That is a woman, no?"

# CHAPTER 18

FROM HIS ROOM in the Arcadia, Ben Cowan went to the offices of General Armijo, only to learn that the General was out. Captain Recalde, despite his wounds, was out also, but he was reported to have gone only as far as the edge of town to interview some peons who had seen some riders. No one remained who had authority to provide Ben Cowan with a horse, and what money he had was insufficient to buy the kind of horse he needed.

His saddle, rifle, and other gear were still at the hotel, and he went back for them now. He settled his bill quickly and carried his gear into the street. The first person he saw as he emerged from the hotel was Rosita Calderon.

She was riding sidesaddle on a magnificent brown gelding, and wore a gray riding habit, her wide skirt spread over the saddle and the flank of the horse. Two vaqueros in buckskin suits and wide sombreros rode with her.

"A horse?" she said. "But of course, señor! You have a horse! Diego bought one for you—a present." She turned and spoke quickly to one of the vaqueros, and the man wheeled his horse and raced away.

"Where will you go now?"

He looked up at her. "I must find those men. They are my responsibility, after all. I must find them and see that the President's treasure is returned, as it should be."

"General Armijo will find them. He is a very good man, the General."

"I know Catlow, and he will do what is not expected of him." Ben Cowan had given a good deal of thought to just what Catlow would do, and he explained as much to Rosita Calderon. Then, seeing her eyes returning to the scratches on his face, he explained that, too.

She laughed. "It is a good explanation. Must I believe it?" Her eyes danced with amusement. "Maybe you were making love to her."

"Do you think a girl I was making love to would scratch that hard?"

She gathered her reins and looked down at him. "I do not know, señor. I know very little of what a girl might do if she were in love, but—I think she would have to love very much, hate very much, or want very much, to scratch like that!"

The vaquero galloped up, leading a brown gelding, the twin of the one Rosita rode—a truly magnificent horse.

"He is yours, Señor Ben. Diego bought him from our ranch as a present to you, who lost your horse in saving his life."

"I was saving my own, too."

"You refuse the horse?"

"Indeed I don't! That's the finest-looking horse I ever did see. No, I'll keep him. I could never refuse an animal as beautiful as that!"

Rosita's eyes sparkled. "It would be safe, I think. Horses do not scratch."

Rosita Calderon looked dashing and lovely on her brown gelding as she smiled at Ben from under the flat brim of her hat. "I think I had better ride along, señor. After all, most of these people you will question know me. Perhaps I can help."

Bijah Catlow, Ben explained, would hit upon the least likely solution; and to escape from Mexico with the treasure, expecting to be pursued, he would be unlikely to take the main trail north toward the border. With a pack train he could not hope to outrun his pursuers.

To go deeper into Mexico to the south would be merely prolonging his task. He might strike for the Sierra Madres and Apache country, or he might strike for the coast. Remembering the Tarahumara Indian, Ben said, "I believe he will try the desert."

Catlow had one great advantage: he knew where he was going. Armijo and Ben Cowan had to discover that . . . and then Catlow could change his apparent destination.

A quick search of the leather shop and the hidden cellar had revealed nothing that was of help. It was evident that a number of men had been there, but now they were gone. Nobody had seen them either come or go, and nobody had seen them while they were there. Christina was gone, too, and so was a fine black horse known to belong to her.

Riding swiftly, stopping only to ask questions, Ben Cowan rode a semicircle around the northern rim of Hermosillo. He ignored the obvious trails the mule train might have taken, but checked all the minor roads and lanes.

An Indian on the outskirts of town offered the first

clue. He had, he told the vaquero who spoke his language, seen nothing. He had gone early to bed, and today he had been busy . . . somebody had left the gate open and flooded his field.

What did he mean by "somebody"? Ben Cowan's questions soon brought out the fact that when the Indian had gone to bed the night before, his orchard had been dry; when he rose in the morning it was flooded.

Acting on a hunch, Ben Cowan circled the orchard. On the far side he found a mule track, almost obliterated by other tracks, and within an hour he had picked up the trail.

At the desert's edge he drew up. "Thank you," he said to Rosita Calderon. "Now you'd best go back. I'll take it from here."

She held out her slender gloved hand. *"Vaya con Dios, señor."* And then she added in English, "And if you come back to Mexico—come to see me."

He watched her straight, slender back as she rode away, then swore softly and turned his horse into the desert.

Forty mules and a dozen mounted horsemen leave some mark upon the land in their passing; and these did so, despite the efforts of Bijah Catlow to keep the trail hidden. The soft sand of washes, the hard-packed sand of windblown mesas, the shallow streambeds—all these were made use of. But always there was the mule that stepped out of line, that trod on vegetation, or left a hoofprint on the edge of a stream.

Ben was a full day behind them when he reached the Bacoachi and saw where they had dug for water. He saw the prints left in the sand where the water kegs had stood while being filled, and he studied what tracks he could find, realizing the knowledge might serve him well at a later time. To a western plainsman, a track was as easily read as a road sign.

From Rosita and the vaqueros he had learned about the country that lay ahead of him. He refilled his two canteens, and when he left the Bacoachi it was dusk and he rode swiftly.

There was no need to see the trail here, for the only water ahead lay at Arivaipa Well in the river bottom of the San Ignacio. If there was no water there, eight miles west at Coyote Wells there might be water.

At midnight Ben made a dry camp, watered his horse from his hat, and, after three hours of rest, saddled up and went on. In the graying light of dawn he found a mule. Or what remained of one.

Played out, the mule had obviously been abandoned, and what happened after that was revealed by the tracks and the bones. The mule had been killed, cooked, and eaten.

Ben Cowan studied the moccasin tracks. They were not Apache or Yaqui, and this was the homeland of the dreaded Seri Indians, said to be cannibals, and known to use poisoned arrows. All sorts of fantastic stories were told about them, most of them untrue. It was sometimes said that they were the descendants of the crew of a Swedish or Norwegian whaler or some other ship wrecked on Tiburon a hundred and fifty years before. At any rate, it was clear that the Seris had come upon the mule and eaten it. There had been a dozen or more in the group.

It was mid-morning when Ben cautiously approached the Pozo Arivaipa. The mule train had been there and had watered, and they had left no water in the well. The bottom of it was merely mud.

He hesitated only an instant. Coyote Wells might be dry, too; and to ride there and back would mean sixteen miles with nothing gained in the pursuit. To the north were the Golondrina *tinajas,* where there would surely be water. They were perhaps twenty-four miles away, with other wells fifteen miles or so beyond.

So Ben Cowan rode north, but he rode uneasily, worried by that half-eaten mule. Those moccasin tracks were surely made by the Seris, and they would be somewhere around; if they lived up to the stories about them they would be up ahead, scouting that mule train.

Did Catlow know? The vaquero who told Ben about the Seris had crossed himself when he mentioned them, and that vaquero was a tough man and a brave one. Ben Cowan rode more slowly, studying the country, and taking care to avoid any likely ambush. He could think of a lot of ways to die, but one he particularly did not want was to turn slowly black with a poisoned arrow in his guts.

He had heard many stories about how that poison was made, none of them appealing. Bartlett, who had led the party that surveyed the border between the United States and Mexico along those miles where New Mexico, Arizona, and California adjoin the Mexican states of Chihuahua, Sonora, and Baja California, reported that the Seris obtained the poison by taking the liver from a cow and putting it in a hole with live rattlesnakes, scorpions, tarantulas, and centipedes, then stirring up the whole mass until the creatures exhausted their venom on each other and on the liver. The arrow points are then passed through this and allowed to dry in the shade.

Father Pfefferkorn, who spent many years in Sonora during the earliest times, had a somewhat different story to tell. The poisons, he said, are collected from all those creatures and also from the Mexican beaded lizard, and mixed with the juices of poisonous plants, then sealed in a large earthenware jar so that none of the poison can evaporate. The pot is then placed on a fire under the open sky and cooked until ready for use. The care of this evil concoction was always delegated to the oldest woman, for when the pot was uncovered the vapor invariably killed her.

Thoughts of such tales as these were in Ben Cowan's mind as he rode.

To the north of the route he was following was the Cerro Prieto, the Black Range, so called because it was covered by dark forest. This was a favorite haunt of the Seris, second only to the Isle of Tiburon.

Ben Cowan rode with caution, his eyes continually busy, not only looking for what the desert could tell him in the way of tracks, but searching the horizon, too. In the desert, the careless die . . . and wherever they are, the reckless die, some sooner, some later. Ben Cowan was neither.

Four miles off to the west, six Seris trotted across the sand. They held to low ground, and they were patient. They knew about Ben Cowan, but they were in no hurry. He was going where they were going, and all in good time they would have him, too. They could afford to wait.

The Seris were of the desert, and the desert can

wait. . . . the buzzard that soars above the desert also knows how to wait. Both desert and buzzard know that sooner or later they will claim most things that walk, creep, or crawl within the desert.

Though the men who drove the mule train were in a great hurry, neither the Seris nor the buzzards were worried. The mule train was marked for death. In fact, death was already among them, and once there, it would not be leaving before its work was done.

Bijah Catlow had seen a mule die . . . and afterward, another mule.

And now a man was to die . . . and then more men.

# CHAPTER 19

UNDER A HOT and smoky sky the mule train stretched out for half a mile, plodding wearily, heavily, exhausted by the distance, the dust, and the everlasting heat. Contorted by the heat, the air quivered and trembled, turning the low areas into pools of water that beckoned with sly, false fingers of hope.

The sky was blazing with the sun of Sonora; though the sun was masked by the smoke from the fires that burned in the hills, there was no relief from the heat. This was the desert . . . sand, rock, cactus, greasewood, and ocotillo . . . and nowhere was there any water.

Bijah Catlow mopped the sweat from his face and blinked at the strung-out train through the sting of the salt sweat in his eyes. He should ride back and make them bunch up; despite all his warnings they did not pay heed to them. It was too far west for Apaches, they claimed, and it was north of Yaqui country; of the Seris, most of them had never heard.

They had watered well at the *tinajas* of Golondrina, but the rock tanks at Del Picu had been bone-dry; so instead of adding another twenty miles to the twelve they had covered, Catlow had turned east toward Pozo del Serna, where there was nearly always water.

Less than an hour ago they had lost the second mule, and had divided its load between five of the others. At the next camp Bijah planned to bunch the supplies that were left, and so free a mule for packing treasure. Though he had expected to lose mules, he had not expected it so soon.

The Tarahumara trotted up to him as Merridew drew up alongside. The Indian spoke rapidly, using sign talk as well. Merridew glanced from him to Catlow. "What's he say?"

"He says we're bein' followed."

Merridew spat. "Well, why don't he tell us somethin' we don't know?"

"He says it isn't white men—it's Seris. And he's scared."

Merridew looked at the Indian. He did look scared, come to think of it. The Old Man's bleak eyes studied the distance, which revealed nothing—only the dancing heat waves, and faint haze of smoke that hung over everything. But he knew the desert too well to be deceived by the apparent emptiness. If that Indian said there were Seris out there, they were there.

The Old Man's horse, carrying much less weight than Bijah's own, was in better shape. "Ride back and bunch them up, will you?" Bijah said to him. "Tell 'em it's not far to water."

He gestured toward the mountains. "It's up there, maybe three, four miles. . . . Then you come back up here—bring Rio or Bob along and we'll scout those wells."

Catlow watched while the riders bunched the mules, scanning the desert at intervals. He had an odd sense of impending disaster that worried him.

From the slight knoll on which he sat his horse, he watched the Old Man ride up with Rio Bray. The three turned their horses eastward then, and cantered forward toward the dark, looming mountains. The low mountains to the right were bare, but to the left and north the crests were covered with a thick forest of pine.

The springs, when they reached them, lay in the bottom of a branch off a dry wash, surrounded by ironwood and smoke trees. In the trees, birds sang; all else was still.

The Tarahumara came up, drank briefly and then disappeared among the trees.

"If there's anybody around," Catlow said, "he'll find 'em."

Rio Bray stepped down from his saddle and drank, then filled his canteen. "How much farther, d'you reckon?"

"Hundred miles."

Bray indicated the mules. "They ain't gonna make it."

"We'll have to get more."

Bray said nothing, but his expression was sour. Bijah swung down and eased the girth on his saddle, then led his horse to the water. Old Man Merridew was doing the same thing.

Suddenly, Rio swore viciously, and kicked a rock.

Catlow glanced up and spoke mildly. "Somethin' bitin' you, Rio?"

"We were damn' fools to come by the desert! Why, if we'd come up the trail we could have stole fresh animals all the way along! We'd have been nigh to the border by now."

"And have half the country chasin' you? That Calderon ranch has a reg'lar army on it, an' tough vaqueros. Did you ever tangle with a bunch of hand-picked Sonora vaqueros? Take it from me, and don't."

"Halfway to the border and not a shot fired," the Old Man commented. "Don't seem too bad to me."

The mule train streamed into the hollow and the mules lined up eagerly along the trickle of water that spilled down from the springs and then disappeared in the sand.

Rio Bray stalked off, and stopped to talk to Pesqui-era. Bijah's eyes followed him. "There's trouble," the Old Man commented.

"Old Man," Bijah said, "if anything happens to me, you take this outfit north to Bisani. There's water there, and the ruins of an old church—good place to fort up if you have to. Caborca's to the east of us, but fight shy of it. You head for La Zorra . . . about fif-teen miles. Less than that distance beyond La Zorra, you come up to the Churupates. There'll be mules waiting there. Follow up the bed of the Rio Seco, then cut for the border and the foot of the Baboquivaris."

"You figured mighty close." Merridew drove the cork into his canteen with a blow of his palm. "Any of the rest of them know that route?"

"No . . . but stick to it." Catlow took up a twig. "Old Man, there's troops stationed at Magdalena, and we all saw them. By now the troops at Altar have been alerted, too. If we tried to go the way Bray sug-gested they'd have us in a pocket."

The packs were stripped from the mules, and they were led out and picketed on the grass. Catlow was everywhere, checking their backs for sores, checking their legs and hoofs. Not much farther with this bunch, he realized, but every mile was important now, and every pack.

The Mexican soldier squatted on the sand and put together a small fire. He glanced up at Catlow with an odd expression in his eyes, and Bijah was instantly alert. He raised his eyes and without turning his head or seeming especially interested, he placed every man—all but Pesquiera.

Rio Bray stood up and two of the Tucson crowd were also standing, spread out from Bray.

"I figure," Rio said, "we should go east, up the Pedradas."

"No," Catlow replied quietly, "we'd be walkin' into a trap." His eyes went slowly around the group, pinning each man. *Where the hell was Pesquiera?*

Keleher got to his feet slowly, suddenly aware of a showdown.

"We talked it over," Rio said, "and we've had enough of goin' short on water. We've decided to take off up the Pedradas."

"You've '*decided*'? Rio, you decide nothing here. What's decided will be decided by me."

Rio's eyes flickered, and Bijah knew where Pesquiera was. On his right, Old Man Merridew held his rifle in his hands. "Go ahead," Catlow said, "you take care of Pesky, Old Man. Rio's my meat."

Rio Bray began to sweat. He looked at Catlow, and suddenly Bijah was smiling. "It's your play, Rio," he said. "You go with us, or you go for that gun."

A few minutes before, Rio Bray had been sure and confident. He had been looking forward to this showdown, and he had Pesquiera for insurance. Now suddenly there was no insurance.

"We're callin' your hand, Catlow," Bray said. "We put it to a vote, and the most of us want to go up the Pedradas."

"Why, now, Rio, you're gettin' mighty democratic about things. You had you a vote, but without me. And I take it, without the Old Man and some others? Well, I want a show of hands. I want the men who want to go by the Pedradas to stand up."

There was a moment of silence and hesitation and then Jake Wilbur stood up. Kentucky and the Greek had already been standing. Nobody else moved.

"All right, Rio. You heard what I said. You go with us, or go for that gun . . . and that goes for all of you." He stood carelessly. "Looks to me like we can almost double our shares right here, Old Man."

Bob Keleher spoke quietly. "Count me with Catlow, boys."

Rio Bray was tense, then slowly he relaxed. "I'll go along, Bijah. No use us shootin' each other to doll rags just when we're all rich."

"What I say," Bijah replied.

Jake Wilbur unrolled his bed and turned in without a word, and after a minute he was followed by the Greek, and then by Kentucky.

Pesquiera's name was not mentioned, and he did not appear.

Afraid to face Catlow after his plan to kill him had failed, Pesquiera drew back in the brush and went to the horses. For a moment he hesitated, wanting to get a muleload of the loot to take with him, but there was no chance of that. Catlow had known he was out in the brush ready to cut him down the moment Rio drew; and when day came, Catlow would certainly call him on it.

Yet there might still be a chance. Ride to General Armijo, claim he had been held a prisoner in his own home, and had escaped. And tell the General where the outlaws were. He might even come out of it with a reward. As for the treasure, he told himself they would have killed him as soon as they reached the border. He believed this because it was what he would have done in their place.

When they saddled up at daybreak, Pesquiera was gone, and no one spoke his name.

Catlow led off before the sun was up, riding due north toward Bisani, which lay twenty-eight water-less miles across the desert. Rio Bray was sullen, and angry with himself. He should have tried for his gun . . . he had been a fool, and this morning his allies of last night held off.

They found Pesquiera's body lying sprawled in the sand less than a mile from camp, with a poisoned arrow through his throat. His face, neck, and the upper part of his body had already turned black with the effects of the poison. He lay there stripped bare. His clothing had been taken away by the Indians.

There was no need to worry about keeping bunched up now. Every man rode with a rifle in hand, and every eye was on the sandhills around them. Bijah Catlow's throat was tight with apprehension. He had never believed the stories he had heard about the Seris. He believed them now.

Mile after mile passed. The Tarahumara ran at Catlow's stirrup now.

They were well clear of the smoke trees and brush when one of the supply mules suddenly reared up, then collapsed in the trail. An arrow projected from its throat.

Keleher started to turn, but Catlow had seen the arrow, and knew that to stop would be fatal. "Keep going!" he shouted, and Keleher swung back to the end of the train.

"Move 'em!" Catlow yelled. "Faster!"

Shouting, and cracking the mules with ropes, they speeded up the train. Catlow and Old Man Merridew galloped back to help Keleher at the drag end of the line.

As they reached the rear of the train, two Indians broke from the sand where they had somehow concealed themselves and ran toward the dying mule, their knives in their hands. Already the nearest mule was a hundred yards from them.

The Old Man raced his horse toward them, and as the Indians leaped up, he fired. The nearest Indian screamed and plunged forward, falling over the dead mule.

Suddenly a dozen Indians broke from the sand within a few yards of the Old Man, and Catlow, slapping spurs to his horse, raced toward them, firing with his Colt. An arrow whipped by his face, and then the Indians were gone, disappearing among the low hills.

Merridew, his face sickly yellow, came up alongside Catlow. "Let's get out of here!" Catlow said.

They had gone less than a mile when Kentucky dropped back from the flank of the mule train.

"Bijah"—he motioned toward the desert to the west—"they're still out there. I just saw one."

Only a few minutes later Bijah saw another, on the other side of the mule train, keeping abreast of it but a good four hundred yards off.

The day grew hot; shadows disappeared. Again the smoke cast a haze across the sun, across the distance where mirage tantalized with its shimmering lakes. The long marches were telling on the horses, and some of the mules were lagging more than ever. The mule train slowed to a walk.

Rio Bray was avoiding Bijah, but he worked as hard as any man to keep the train moving. There was no thought of pausing at noon. They had only one thought now—of reaching Bisani. They had even forgotten General Armijo, and his soldiers who would be riding all the trails, searching for them.

With every mile the danger became greater, but the border drew nearer; and among the weird rocks of the Churupates they would find fresh mules and horses awaiting them, ready for a fast march to the border.

They knew that the Indians were all around them. At times they heard weird calls from the distance, strange singsong sounds from the sandhills. But they saw no one. The Indians never showed themselves, but from time to time their signals to one another sounded across the desert.

Another mule went down, struggled to get up, then stayed down. Ringed by rifles, two of the men stripped the pack and packsaddle from the animal and distributed the load among the others. Then they started on, but only a few minutes later the mule was up and following them on wobbly legs.

Before the first shadow appeared on the eastern flank of a hill, three more mules had gone down—one of them did not rise again.

Now the going was very slow, for all the remaining mules were overloaded.

Catlow rode toward the top of a rise. A coarse stubble of beard covered his face, and his shirt was stiff with sweat and dust. He mounted the ridge, and there, beside the dry bed of Asuncion River, was the ruined church of Bisani. Among the ruins he could see the flickering green leaves of a poplar—almost a sure indication of water.

"Here it is!" he called. "We're safe!"

From behind him came a ragged cheer.

# CHAPTER 20

DEPUTY UNITED STATES Marshal Ben
Cowan had no need to trace the trail left by
the fleeing outlaws and their mule train, for the route
was marked by circles of flying buzzards.

From a low ridge crowned with rocks and a clump
of elephant trees, Cowan studied the desert before
him through his field glasses. He liked the spicy odor
of the small trees, and they offered a limited but welcome bit of shade. Nearby the brown gelding cropped
at some desert plants.

That the mule train was under attack was obvious.
He could hear the distant sound of guns and could see
racing horsemen, although where he sat he was too
far off for him to identify any individual rider. Nor
could he see the attacking Indians.

He watched the fleeing mule train and its accom-
panying riders. Suddenly a rider went down and
others raced to his aid. There was a flurry of shots
and white smoke lifting, and then they were racing
off again with, he surmised, the rescued man.

The shooting continued, sporadic firing at targets
invisible to him. It gave him a strange sensation to sit
as at a show and watch men fighting for their lives
against a ghostlike enemy. As for the Indians, he had
no need to be on the spot to understand their strat-
egy. They were following the mule train like wolves

after a crippled animal, attacking, escaping, returning to attack again.

Mounting up, Ben Cowan turned his horse eastward, away from the fight. Obviously, Catlow was pointing toward a destination that could not be far off. Otherwise he would stand and make a fight of it. Topping another rise, Ben saw what they were heading for. Before him opened a wide vista of green fields, long deserted and converted by nature to pasture land. Beyond lay the river, and on higher ground nearby he saw a cluster of ruined walls and arches, and a few trees.

Suddenly, his horse snorted and shied.

Ben looked around swiftly, in time to see a Seri Indian step from the brush and draw his bow. Ben's right hand chopped down and swept up. The gun leaped in his hand and his bullet struck the Indian an instant before the arrow was released. The arrow shot away above Ben's head, and he saw the Indian falling. Abruptly, he leaped his horse between two trees. An Indian rose from the ground in front of him, and Ben saw his face writhe with horror as the forehoofs of the charging horse struck him.

Plunging free of the brush, Ben Cowan saw Indians springing up behind him, and he raced away toward the ruined walls. Even as he rode for sanctuary from the east, Catlow and his mule train came across the abandoned fields from the south. And none of them were prepared for what happened.

Ben Cowan, racing across the fields, caught a glint of sun on a rifle barrel, and with a shock of horror he realized that the fleeing bandits, escaping from the Indians, were charging into the waiting guns of an ambuscade.

Now he could see them, a dozen Mexicans in wide sombreros crouched behind the walls, rifles ready, and standing over them a woman . . . *Christina!*

There was no time to think, no time for a choice. His Colt was in his hand, and lifting it, he fired. The shot struck near one of the waiting Mexicans and he jerked back with an oath just as Ben Cowan leaped his horse over the low outer wall of the enclosure.

The bulk of the ruin was now between him and the outlaws, and he dropped from his horse and, hitting the ground running, dove for shelter among the rocks. But even before he left his horse he had seen the riders from the mule train break stride, and when he hit the ground it was with Catlow's wild yell ringing in his ears.

Someone rushed him and he straightened up suddenly, firing at almost point-blank range into the belly of a charging Mexican.

The man struck him full tilt, and Ben was knocked back off his feet, the Mexican on top of him. All around were roaring guns, stabbing flame, and screams of fear or pain. Above it all he could hear the strident screams of Christina as she urged her men in the fight.

Ben threw off the body of the wounded man and lunged up to grapple with another Mexican. In an instant they were rolling on the ground. Then horses were leaping the walls around him, and the ruins of the ancient mission became a shambles.

Pulling free of his man, Ben saw the fellow grasp the hilt of his knife, and Ben's fist was swinging. The blow caught the Mexican with the knife half drawn, and he hit the ground as if struck with an axe.

And then suddenly the fighting was over. There was the sound of moans, the smell of powder smoke—and Bijah Catlow was grasping him by the hand.

"Man, oh man!" Catlow shouted. "If you hadn't shot to warn us, they'd have mowed us down! You saved our bacon, you old Souwegian, you!"

Old Man Merridew, on one knee behind the wall, fired at a Seri . . . and then there were none in sight.

Cowan looked around him. Christina and four of her hastily recruited Mexican outlaws were prisoners. Three others he saw lying dead on the ground. Two dead mules and a horse lay in the field outside the mission walls, and at least one man—there might be another behind a horse out there. Catlow's force had been cut to seven, including himself. Two horses were standing in the field.

Catlow went to his horse and stepped into the saddle. "Cover me," he said; "I'm going to have a look. Maybe one of the boys is lyin' out there, hurt." And then he added, "While I'm at it, I'll pick up those horses and whatever else."

"I'll ride along," Ben said.

Together they rode out over the field. They walked their horses, and they went warily. There was no cover close by, but the Seris seemed to need none—they could spring from the ground where it seemed no concealment could be.

A man's body was lying half under one of the horses; it was Rio Bray. He had been shot through the skull and through the body.

"He gave me trouble," Catlow said, "but he was a good man to ride with . . . only bullheaded."

They picked up the guns, gathered the horses and canteens. Beside one of the dead mules Catlow stopped to recover the pack.

"Bijah, why don't you surrender to me? You haven't got a chance, you know."

"What gives you that idea?"

"If Christina could make it here, General Armijo could."

"Nothin' doin'. Anyway, we ain't out of this fix yet. There's no water inside those walls, and there's plenty of Indians outside."

Back within the walls, Catlow dismounted, and glanced around at the loafing men. "All right—get busy. First off, you strip the gear from the horses and mules and give each of them a rubdown. Work on 'em good. We may have to run for it to get out of here."

"How far to the border?" Keleher asked.

"As the crow flies? Eighty miles. Rough miles, if you ask me. . . . Next, you boys clean your guns. Scatter around the walls and keep a sharp eye out. We ain't fresh out of Indians, you can bet."

Bijah took his hat off and wiped the sweatband, and dropped to a seat with his back against the inner wall of the ruined church. Under his breath he whispered to Cowan.

"Ben, if you get shut of this place, I've got a mess of horses waitin' in the Churupates, about thirty miles northwest o' here. Nobody knows but me an' the Old Man. Horses and mules."

They sat there quietly. Nearby were the prisoners,

and three wounded men—one of Catlow's and two of the bandits recruited by Christina.

"I'd watch that one," Ben said, with a slight gesture toward Christina. "She's got no more conscience than a rattler, and she's just as mean."

"Her?" Catlow laughed. "That there's quite a girl. You just seen the wrong side of her."

Then he grew serious. "Damn it, Ben, why didn't I tell Cord the truth? That there's a woman, you know?"

"I think so."

"If I ever get out of this . . ."

"You'd have to go straight."

"Who'd want it any other way? Anyway," he said, "just let me over the border and I'll buy her a piece of Oregon she couldn't ride across in a week."

He got up and delegated some of the men to sleep while others kept watch. There was no cover close to the ruins except on the side of the riverbank, and even then, not much. Then he returned to the place near Cowan and, without another word, stretched out and in a moment was asleep.

Ben Cowan sat beside him for a few minutes, considering the situation. There was no telling how many Indians were out there—there might be few or there might be many. But now the Indians had their chance to bottle them up good.

He glanced at the cottonwoods. There ought to be water here. Had the monks who had lived in this place gone to the river for their water? It did not seem logical. There had been trouble with the Seris in their time, too; and though at first the Seri Indians had yielded many converts, later they had left the fold, perhaps with reason, and had become relentless foes of the Spanish.

Ben got to his feet and slowly scouted the ruins. At one point, in a hollow not far from the wall, he saw a low place where the grass grew thick and green. He went to the packs and got a shovel, and returned to the spot.

Outlining a space about four feet in diameter, he sank the spade in. For several minutes he dug, but the earth was dry. Nobody came near him, and when he had the hole down two feet he put the shovel aside and went back to Catlow. He was still asleep.

Two of the men had started fires, and one was making coffee, the other broiling some mule meat. Nobody spoke to Ben, and he went over to where Christina sat. Her wrists and ankles were tied and she shot him a venomous look, but he merely smiled.

"I should have killed you!" she said.

"You tried," he said. "I'll say that you tried."

He squatted on his heels beside her. "You shouldn't have come," he said. "None of us may get out of this alive. Those Seris, they can wait. They can wait for weeks if they want to—we can't." He paused for a moment, then added, "There isn't food enough— even if we could get water."

Then he left her and returned to the hole and dug again for several minutes. At the end of the time the bottom looked the same.

When he went back to the place by the wall, Catlow had left it. The men had exchanged places, and those who had been on guard slept. Catlow came toward him, a cup of coffee in one hand, and strip of jerked beef in the other.

"Never fancied mule meat. Apaches like it better than beef." He bit off a chunk of the beef and worked at it seriously for several minutes.

"Old Man, he was a mountain man—trapped with Carson, Bridger, and them. He says the best meat of all is puma—mountain lion. Says Coulter told him the Lewis and Clark men preferred it to all other meat. He tried it many a time, swears it's best."

When he had finished eating, Catlow cleaned his rifle and reloaded it, and Cowan did the same. Neither man talked much, and from around the walls the low murmur of conversation was slowly petering out. Not a man but expected an attack. They could not guess whether it would be a screaming rush out of the darkness, or a creeping menace, sliding ever closer to the walls under cover of darkness.

Seated against the wall, Ben Cowan tried to compose himself for sleep, but the face of Rosita as he had last seen her kept coming into his thoughts. And when sleep came Rosita was still in his mind.

Darkness fell, the fires died . . . a sleeping man muttered, and somewhere a coyote howled.

Ben Cowan woke with a start, and for a moment he held himself perfectly still. Never in his life had he awakened as he had now, filled with such a sense of dread.

He lowered his hand for his gun . . . and it was not there.

# CHAPTER 21

H E LAY STILL, sorting out the situation in his mind. Carefully, he felt around on the ground, but he was sure the gun had not fallen of itself, but had been taken from his holster. The gun was gone.

He sat up, careful to make no sound. Bijah might have taken it, but that he doubted. Or one of the others might have done it, knowing him for a United States Marshal. Yet that, too, he doubted.

The pistol was gone, and his rifle was gone, and whoever had taken them must be incredibly light-fingered. *Christina?*

He got to his feet, and stood listening. The night was still, incredibly still, when one came to think of it.

No one but Bijah had slept near him. Ben's eyes grew accustomed to the night, and he stepped over to where Bijah lay. He bent over him, shaking him gently. Bijah was instantly awake.

Bending down, Ben whispered, "You got your gun?"

Bijah's hand moved, felt. "No! What the—"

"Ssh!" He leaned closer. "Mine's gone, too. Where's Christina?"

Together, they stepped to the break in the wall. All was dark and still. A man turned and muttered in his sleep.

Bijah went quickly to where Christina had been left, Ben Cowan close behind him. *She was gone!*

The other prisoners were gone, too.

Swiftly, silently, the camp was awakened. Every man had been stripped of his guns. The two sentries were dead—they had been strangled. Old Man Merridew had been struck over the head, apparently as he awakened.

Crouching together, every man realized what must have happened. Christina had freed herself, then her men. And then she, moving with the softness of a cat, had gone from one to the other, stripping them of their guns. The Old Man had started to wake up and had been struck; the guards had undoubtedly been strangled without ever realizing what was happening.

"Now what?" Keleher asked.

"The Seris," someone said, "they'll be comin'."

"That's what she figured," Bijah said quietly. "Oh, she's a smart one! When the soldiers found us, we'd all be dead, killed by the Seris . . . the loot gone. And they'd never even look for it again, figuring the Indians had it."

"Look funny, us dead with no guns," one of the men said. "Hell," said another one, "they'd bring those back and scatter them around! And they'd take off with the loot, scot-free!"

"That ain't the question," Bijah interrupted. "Them Seris'll be comin'. We've got to fight."

Ben Cowan spoke up. "Maybe they won't come. Gather all the fuel you can. Get some fires going."

"Huh?" Bijah looked up at him in amazement.

"Indians are puzzled by anything they don't understand—hell, anybody is! So we build fires and we keep them going all night. We make noise around, lots of confusion so they don't know exactly what's happening, and maybe they'll hold off. Meanwhile, we rig any sort of weapons we can find that will help us fight them off."

Bijah went immediately to the remains of the fire, stirred the coals, then put on fuel. Dead branches and brush lay about, and there were two dead trees. All these were gathered. A second fire was started, and in a few minutes the flames were a roaring blaze.

All of the men but one had knives. Bijah had a derringer he had kept as a hideaway gun. Several of the men began making spears whose points they hardened in the fires. Loose bricks and stones were gathered. Some of the men slipped off their socks—a stone in the end of a sock could be used for a club.

Meanwhile they shouted, sang, banged sticks together, and ran back and forth, never stopping where they might offer a target. It was a mad, unbelievable sight, but the men caught the spirit of it and it soon became almost a game. Wild yells rang out, shrill cowboy yells, and Indian warwhoops.

When the stars began to pale, Bijah spoke to the men. "All right—saddle up and load up. We're goin' to ride out of here."

"Them Indians are out there!"

"Sure they are. But have they ever attacked us close up? We'll ride out of here carryin' sticks to look like guns. We'll ride out with our loot and we'll head northwest. We'll ride like hell the first few miles to get ahead of the Indians, then we'll troop along for a ways, then ride hard again. There'll be fresh horses waiting for us when we get there."

"Don't forget," Merridew said, "that woman is out there with her men and our guns."

"How could I forget that?" Bijah said bitterly. "We'll just have to gamble on her."

Their water supply was scanty, and suddenly Ben thought of the hole he had dug. Turning, he went to the corner of the enclosure, and there it was—filled with water! Not enough for them all, but enough to water the horses and some of the mules.

They waited until almost daylight for more water to seep into the hole, and it did come in, but not very rapidly. By the time they were ready to move, there was enough to water the rest of the animals. The men themselves would have to get along on whatever water they had in their canteens, and it was precious little.

They rode out of the walls in a close bunch, down into the streambed and across it. Once on the other side, Bijah gave the word and they rode out at a rapid clip.

They saw nothing, they heard nothing. Morning lay gray upon the landscape. A light breeze drifted across the desert, played fitfully among the cactus, and died out. Carrying their sticks like rifles, the small band kept up the pace.

With Ben Cowan added to Catlow's band, there were eight of them. Catlow's wounded man was able to ride, and to some extent, to fight. There was also one wounded man from Christina's group, the other one having died during the night. Pancho, the Mexican who had brought the news to Catlow in Tucson, had proved one of the best men he had.

After galloping the horses for almost a mile, Bijah

slowed down to a trot. There was no sign of the Indians. The Seris had never shown any indication that they would attack a ready and courageous enemy, but if the least sign of weakness or fear was indicated they would attack like madmen. That they were out there watching them, neither Ben nor Bijah had any doubt.

They kept on, and gradually the ground began to rise. When they reached a comparatively level place, all but the wounded dismounted and walked their horses to rest them.

Ben swore softly at being without a gun. He carried a bowie knife, but that was good only at close quarters. He knew that if once the sharp-eyed Seris detected that the riders were without rifles they would attack. They would not need to come to close quarters; they could stand off fifty or sixty yards and shoot them down with arrows.

"Where d'you suppose that woman got to?" Bijah said suddenly. "How'd she manage to slip out without them catching her?"

But Ben had no answer to this.

The day wore on, the sun climbed higher in the sky, the dreadful Sonora heat came upon them. The last of their water went to the wounded, and miles yet lay before them. The exhausted mules slowed and wanted to stop, but they drove them on ruthlessly. Now they could see, looming above the mirage, a far-off peak. "The Churupates," Bijah said, and they rode with hope.

Ben Cowan's mouth was dry and his head ached from the heat. He loosened his shirt buttons, and squinted his eyes against the salt of the sweat on his face. The good brown gelding went steadily on, but now and then a heavily laden mule staggered.

The wounded Mexican muttered in delirium, and moaned for water, but now there was none to give him. Dust rose in their faces, heat waves shimmered before their eyes. Around them grew creosote bush and cactus, along with the ever-present ocotillo. Otherwise the desert was empty.

Mules stopped and had to be whipped to move them along, for to stop here, whether the Seris attacked or not, meant death. They plodded through a weird hell of cactus and heat, a world in which nothing seemed to exist but themselves.

Suddenly off in the distance toward the east, Ben saw a column of riders. "Look!" he cried.

"Five of them," Bijah said bitterly. "That's Christina."

"We've fooled them, too," Ben said after a moment. "They think we've got rifles. If they didn't, they would move in and shoot us down."

"Maybe you're right."

"I don't think so," the Old Man said wryly. "We're headin' for somewhere, an' she's got an idea what it's for—horses and mules. We're safe until we get there, because she'll need that stock as bad as we do."

The miles unwound behind them. The wounded Mexican raved and screamed hoarsely, crying and begging for water. A mule went down, and they shifted its pack to the others and moved on, leaving it lying there.

Bijah Catlow mopped his chest and swore, turning his eyes toward the distant mountain. The Mexican, Pancho, caught his shoulder and pointed excitedly at a dark loom of cloud beyond the mountain. *"Tiempo de agua!"* he shouted.

"Hell," Bijah said, "he's right! This here's beginnin' the rainy period. Last of July, through August and September, it rains nearly every day. The trouble is, they're just local rains and may not reach us at all. If you've got any influence upstairs, Ben, you'd better pray. We're goin' to need that water before we make the Churupates."

The cloud mounted rapidly, and in the distance thunder rumbled. The far-off cloud was split by a streak of lightning. A faint, cool breeze stirred the desert, and the animals staggered on.

Bijah carried his derringer almost all the time now, ready in his hand so it could be used immediately. Twice Indians had appeared not far off.

Ben was scared, and he admitted it to himself. No gun—only a knife, and the Indians closing in. Once it dawned on the Seris that they were unarmed—and if they got closer they could see that—they would be upon them.

That distant peak of the Churupates seemed no closer. But the wind blew a cooling breath from off the mountains, and the horses perked up, and the mules, too.

Thunder rolled continuously now, lightning flashed, and the wind blew harder. And then the rain came. It came with a rush, the dreaded *culebra de agua,* or water snake, which will flood villages, devastating the countryside. They scrambled across a dry wash and up the other side, and behind them came a rushing turmoil of water that filled the wash.

Holding in a tight bunch, they pushed on. Once

they stopped to allow the animals to drink a little at one of the pools on the desert. The animals seemed to have gained new strength, but the lashing rain and roaring thunder wiped out everything but the storm itself and the driving necessity to go on.

For more than an hour the rain came in a veritable cloudburst. Then it eased off, although it continued for almost two hours more. Finally it eased away, leaving the desert drenched and cool. When the clouds cleared, the Churupates were just ahead.

Bijah Catlow had fallen behind, and Ben lagged behind with him. As the outlaws and their mule train crossed the hill that was the beginning of the Churupates, Ben rode out on one flank to push a mule back into the herd. He heard a clatter of hoofs and looked around to see Catlow disappearing up an arroyo, driving several of the mules ahead of him. He hesitated only a moment then wheeled his horse and rode after him.

He could have gone no more than a hundred yards when the arroyo branched, and the light was too dim to see tracks. Catlow and at least four mules had vanished. Cowan hesitated, chose the wrong arroyo and, after riding a short distance, started back. Bijah was waiting for him in the main arroyo when he reached it.

Only when he was abreast of him could Cowan see that Catlow was grinning. "Fooled, weren't you?" He chuckled. "I believe in a little insurance. The way our luck's been runnin', I don't trust that place up there."

They rode over the hill, then around a bluff. There, in a hollow among the hills of the Churupates was a ruined cabin and a small corral. At pasture in the hollow were the mules and horses awaiting them. But there was something more.

The last light of day showed the scene in the hollow, though against the far wall it was dark. In the center were the outlaws, their hands lifted; around them and all around the hollow there must have been at least two hundred horsemen . . . Mexican soldiers.

Instantly, Ben Cowan whipped the cuffs from his belt, and before Bijah could grasp the situation, snapped one around his wrist, the other around the pommel.

"What the hell!" Bijah burst out in a fury. "You damned Judas, you'd—"

"Shut up, you hotheaded fool!" Ben said quickly. "You're my prisoner—unless you'd rather rot in a Mexican jail, which you justly deserve."

Bijah started to open his mouth to speak again, then he closed it tight. After a minute, he said, "You damned fool," but he said it with affection.

# CHAPTER 22

"YOU UNDERSTAND, OF course," General Armijo said coolly, "we need not let you have these prisoners?"

"I understand," Cowan replied. "Of course, they were my prisoners. I was bringing them in—and the treasure."

"So it seems—and, of course, we do have the treasure. Or most of it. You lost several mules, my scouts report."

"There was no opportunity to recover the treasure," Ben Cowan replied, honestly enough. "And not much of it was lost."

Armijo stood up. "We have much to thank you for," he said quietly, "so the prisoners shall be yours. It was your warning that alerted us, and the treasure was recovered by you. Also, there is the matter of Captain Recalde, whose life you saved."

"It was little enough to do."

Armijo thrust out his hand. "Very well, señor. *Vaya con Dios!*"

Ben Cowan went down the steps and into the street. His prisoners, roped together, stood waiting for him. The two Mexicans stood to one side, under separate guard.

He went to them. To the Mexican who had ridden with Bijah, he said, "I could do nothing for you, although I tried. Nor for you," he said to the other. "You are Mexican nationals, and I had no claim upon you as prisoners."

Pancho shrugged. "It is nothing, señor. It is the way of fortune. The Army or prison, does it matter?" He smiled. "I think it will be the Army. I am a good soldier, and the General, he knows this. He will say much, there will be the guardhouse, but then I shall be a soldier again. You will see."

Ben Cowan checked his pockets for money. Little enough was left. "I'm taking you boys back on the stage," he said to the men, "but all I can do is pay your fare to Tucson. If you eat, you'll have to feed yourselves."

"I'm wearin' a money belt," Bijah said, "an' you might as well help yourself. What's the fare by stage?"

"Ten dollars per head, from here."

"I'll pay my own way. If I'm headin' for jail I might as well go in style."

They could see the church at Fronteras for some time before they reached the town. The church was built on the very brow of a hill, with the town scattered around it, and the houses—most of them ruined adobes—were built along the side of the hill.

When the stage rolled into town, Ben Cowan stepped down and looked around carefully. The first person he saw was Rosita Calderon.

On this day it was a black horse she rode, an animal as fine as the brown. Her white buckskin skirt was draped over its side. Her yellow silk blouse showed off her olive skin, and her black hair and eyes to striking effect.

"How did you get here?" he asked, startled by her unexpected appearance.

"We have a ranch near Fronteras, and I came north with my father. It is much faster by carriage, and on the main trail."

The cramped prisoners had slowly been unloading from the stagecoach. All wore handcuffs.

"If we can be of assistance, my vaqueros are nearby," Rosita said.

"Thanks, no. All we want to do is eat and keep rolling."

Her eyes were enigmatic. "You leave Mexico, then?"

"I must take them back."

"I—we shall be sorry to see you go. You have many friends in Sonora."

He looked up at her. "It is time for me to go. If I were to remain, I might forget that I am only a man with a horse and a gun."

"My ancestor," she said quietly, "who first came to Mexico, came with Cortez. He was only a man with a horse and a sword . . . he founded a family."

Ben hesitated, for he was a man of few words, and unaccustomed to women. "I am a gringo," he said, "and the badge I wear is all I have."

"In New Mexico," Rosita said gently, "I have a cousin, whose name was Drusilla Alvarado. She married a gringo who wore a badge . . . she is very happy, señor."

Ben Cowan looked down at his boot toes. He looked up the street and down the street, and then he looked up at her, and thought nobody had ever lived who was so beautiful. He said, "I'll come back."

He turned quickly toward the restaurant, then stopped and looked around. "And I won't be gone long!"

He led them all inside and seated them and ordered bull beef for them, with frijoles and tortillas and plenty of coffee. He had no appetite himself. He just sat there staring out of the window.

Bijah Catlow looked at him. "Ben, I swear I never saw the like. The most beautiful girl in Sonora, an' you almost muffed it! I'd a notion to slug you!"

"Shut up," Ben said, politely.

When he had herded them out to the waiting stage he felt for the derringer. That hideaway gun he had taken from Bijah was the only weapon he had . . . but he would need no other for these men as long as he was in Mexico. They all knew what would happen if they escaped in Mexico, and were captured again.

They were handcuffed two by two except for Bijah, and on him Ben had leg irons as well. Bijah was rather proud of them and kept showing them off. "Figures I'm a dangerous man," he would say, grinning. "Either that, or mighty fast afoot."

It might have been the last thing he ever said. He said it to a girl and her mother who were also waiting for the stage, and when he said it he was not looking around. That was why he did not see the man standing on the corner some fifty feet away.

"I told you," the cold voice cut in, "that I'd choose the time."

Bijah turned around and looked at Miller, who was standing there with a gun in his hand, and he was smiling.

If Miller saw the girl on the horse who rode slowly

down the street toward them, he paid no attention. She was a stranger, and he had no reason to think of her.

Ben Cowan stepped out on the street, and Miller had reason to think of him, but Ben wore no gun-belt, and there was no gun tucked into his waistband. Ben thought of the derringer in his pocket, useless at the distance, and for the first time he knew what despair was. He had been frightened in his time, but he had never known despair; but he knew the sort of man he faced, and Bijah was in irons and helpless, and so was he, without a gun.

Miller knew it. "You too, Marshal? Well, why not?"

Rosita Calderon had grown up on a cow ranch, and the horse she rode was a good cutting horse that was a fast starter. She touched him with a spur and he lunged into a dead run from a walking start. His powerful haunches seemed to squat and he was off, charging like a bullet.

Miller saw her, but his attention was concentrated on the men before him. If he thought anything, it was only that she was somebody trying to get out of the way.

*"Ben!"*

At the cry, Miller's eyes turned briefly. Ben reached up and snared the flying, shining object that came spinning toward him. He caught it in mid-air, as he had caught many a gun doing the border shift, and the .44 Colt struck his palm solidly, his fingers closing around it. He saw the startled fear in Miller's eyes, and saw flame burst from the muzzle of Miller's gun, and then Ben Cowan was walking in firing. He must, at all costs, keep Miller's gun on him. Not a shot must be fired at Catlow, who could not fight back.

Miller was a cornered wolf. He felt a bullet smash his hip and he went down; felt a bullet whiff past his head. He took dead aim and saw dust leap from Ben Cowan's jacket.

Then he felt a violent blow on the skull and he fell back against the porch post, to which he clung, a blazing light in his brain. Squinting his eye, he lifted the gun and felt something smash into his chest, drawing a clear thread of pain through him. His gun hammered into the dust, and he watched the tiny spurts of dust leap from the street in front of him. He kept on clinging to the post with one arm and holding the gun with the other, and he had no idea that he was dead.

Ben Cowan swayed on his feet, and a curious weakness in his knees made them give way. He fell forward, losing his grip on the silver-plated, ivory-handled gun.

For a long moment there was silence in the street, and then Bijah Catlow shuffled forward and, stooping, went into Ben Cowan's pocket for the keys to his irons. First he unfastened the handcuffs, then the leg irons. Then he took up the silver-mounted gun and holstered it.

When he looked up he looked into a Winchester in the hands of Rosita Calderon. It was aimed right between his eyes, and he knew she would shoot.

"Ma'am," he said, "you don't need that. We're goin' to fix this gent up, you an' me, and then we're all goin' over the border so he can turn us in."

He unpinned the badge from Cowan's chest. "I'll just wear this here and appoint myself deputy, so it'll all be official."

———

BEN COWAN WAS looking out of the window for a long time before he realized it. His eyes had opened on a sunlit vista; a lace curtain was stirring gently in the softest of breezes, and he had a feeling of tremendous comfort and complete lassitude such as he had never known before.

The bed was the biggest bed he had ever slept in, and it was the first time he had ever looked out a window with lace curtains.

When he had been lying there for some time watching horses playing on the green field, the oddity of it began to worry him. What could he be doing in such a place? What had happened to him?

Behind him a door opened and when he turned his head he looked into a pair of wide, startled black eyes. He heard an astonished squeal and then the middle-aged Mexican woman was running away, calling to someone.

When he looked around again at the sound of footsteps, he looked into the eyes of Rosita Calderon.

He rolled on his back, clasped his hands behind his head, and smiled up at her. "First time I ever received a lady, lyin' in bed," he said.

A faint flush showed under the olive of her skin. "Maria," Rosita said, "you had better see to him yourself. I think the señor is recovering more rapidly than we expected."

He was sitting up eating a bowl of soup when Bijah Catlow came in. He was wearing the badge.

Cowan looked at it skeptically. "Where'd that come from?"

"It's yours," Catlow said cheerfully. He shoved his hat on the back of his head and hung his thumbs in his belt. "Figured it would look better, me takin' your prisoners over the border to turn them in."

"You took them over?"

"Sure did."

"Who'd you turn them over to?"

"Well"—Bijah's forehead wrinkled with an expression of mock worry—"that there part bothered me some. I didn't rightly know who to turn them over to, so I went to sleep studyin' about it; and you know, when I woke up they were gone! The whole kit an' kaboodle of them!"

Ben ate soup in silence.

After a minute, Bijah said quietly, "So far's I knew, you had nothing on them, anyway. Not in the States. When they got away it was down near Pete Kitchen's place. I figured the only prisoner you really had anything on was me. And here I am."

Ben finished his soup. "Bijah, I'm going to be here a while. You give me that star, and you ride to El Paso and turn yourself in to the office of the U.S. Marshal there. There's a man there temporarily at least, and he'll handle your case. You do that, d'you hear?"

"Sure." Catlow unpinned the badge. "Liable to get myself shot wearin' that, anyway."

Two weeks later, while Ben Cowan was sitting on

the porch at the Hacienda Calderon, Rosita placed a letter in his hand.

> *El Paso*
>
> *Dear Ben:*
> *I take pen in hand to inform you we are all pleesed to heer you are comin along fine. Abijah Catlow, on the Wanted List, showed up here and said you said he was to turn himself in. He done it.*
>
> *He also handed us your report on Miller. He also handed us a paper from Miller's pocket locatin the Army payroll stole by Miller. Most of it recovered.*
>
> *Yrs. Trly,*
> *Will T. Lasho, Dep.*
>
> *P.S. Catlow broke jail. Aint seen hide nor hair of him.*

The first came a year later, from Malheur County, in Oregon.

It said simply: *We named the first one Ben.*

And down Sonora way a boy rides the range whose name is Abijah.

# What Is Louis L'Amour's Lost Treasures?

Louis L'Amour's Lost Treasures is a project created to release some of the author's more unconventional manuscripts from the family archives.

Currently included in the project are *Louis L'Amour's Lost Treasures: Volume 1,* published in the fall of 2017, and *Volume 2,* which will be published in the fall of 2019. These books contain both finished and unfinished short stories, unfinished novels, literary and motion picture treatments, notes, and outlines. They are a wide selection of the many works Louis was never able to publish during his lifetime.

In 2018 we will release *No Traveller Returns,* L'Amour's never-before-seen first novel, which was written between 1938 and 1942. In the future, there may be a selection of even more L'Amour titles.

Additionally, many notes and alternate drafts to Louis's well-known and previously published novels and short stories will now be included as "bonus feature" postscripts within the books that they relate to. For example, the Lost Treasures postscript to *Last of the Breed* will contain early notes on the story, the short story that was discovered to be a missing piece of the novel, the history of the novel's inspiration and creation, and information about unproduced motion picture and comic book versions.

An even more complete description of the Lost Treasures project, along with a number of examples of what is in the books, can be found at louislamourslosttreasures.com. The website also contains a good deal of exclusive material, such as even more pieces of unknown stories that were too short or too incomplete to include in the Lost Treasures books, plus personal photos, scans of original documents, and notes on the Sackett, Chantry, and Talon family series.

All of the works that contain Lost Treasures project materials will display the Louis L'Amour's Lost Treasures banner and logo.

# LOUIS L'AMOUR'S LOST TREASURES

# Postscript

*By Beau L'Amour*

In my father's notes I've come across no information about the writing of *Catlow*. Fortunately, however, I can share some interesting details about the making of the film.

*Catlow* was the second of three Louis L'Amour movies made by British film producer Euan Lloyd. The most important aspect of how these films were created, and the reason I have some stories to include here, is the close relationship that Euan had with my father and our entire family. From the first we were all good friends, and none of the many stressful aspects of the motion picture business could damage that friendship. Unique in the culture of filmmaking, Euan was a man who always tried to be as good as his word. From the time he and my father first met until the day Euan died, in the summer of 2016, he remained the model of a true gentleman.

What my father and Euan attempted to do was new and exciting. They rode a wave of change that was sweeping Hollywood and the culture at large.

They took a lot of chances together, and some of those chances failed to pay off. *Shalako, Catlow,* and *The Man Called Noon* were far from the greatest of films. Their continuing friendship, however, was a testament to their belief and trust in one another. They were both men who knew that to get anywhere in a time of change you had to take risks.

From the mid-1960s to the early 1980s, the motion picture business in the United States evolved dramatically. Competition with television had led to an era of more and more elaborate and expensive theatrical productions. When that trend nearly bankrupted the industry, new alternatives were sought. For a number of reasons, the volume of foreign films released in the US grew, and so did the number of American movies produced, at a significant savings, in foreign countries. The days of the old system, with its "studio-owned" stars, writers, and directors, was over. Both European and American audiences seemed to be looking for something other than the slick and sometimes decadent Hollywood productions that had been a staple of the business since its earliest years. The era of the independent film, made with little or no backing from the production arm of a movie studio and often produced outside the United States, had arrived.

In the arena of Western movies, the best known of this new wave are the so-called Spaghetti Westerns, in particular the three films directed by Sergio Leone and starring Clint Eastwood: *A Fistful of Dollars* (1964), *For a Few Dollars More* (1965), and *The Good, the Bad and the Ugly* (1966). However, between the beginning of the 1960s and the end of the

1970s there were actually hundreds of Westerns made in Europe. With the number of studio films dropping, foreign production was an avenue that even those living in Hollywood had to take seriously.

Louis and Euan were introduced to one another in the early 1960s by film star Alan Ladd. Euan had been a publicist on Ladd's 1953 film *Paratrooper*. When he expressed an interest in production work, Ladd arranged a position for the young Englishman with producers Irving Allen and Albert "Cubby" Broccoli on their next film, *The Black Knight*. From there, Euan worked his way up the ladder, through travel documentaries to more important positions on more important features.

My father and Euan met many times at the Ladds' residence, and before long the two of them were discussing ways to make movies while avoiding the bottleneck and blather that tended to accompany deals made with the major studios. Louis gave Euan a free option (an option is an agreement to "rent" a story until such time as the money can be raised to make the film) on *Shalako*, a story that Euan felt he might be able to cast out of his personal phone book because of its many European characters.

I'll save the story of *Shalako* for another time, but it was an extraordinary example of the art of producing a truly "independent" motion picture. Juggling fantastically creative deals with cast members, financiers, national governments, and distributors in over thirty different countries, Euan somehow managed to patch a production together.

*Catlow* began as a similar attempt. Soon after the

requisite distribution and promotional chores surrounding *Shalako* died down, Euan began the process of hiring the writers to create the new script. Nearly all of 1970 was spent attempting to lock in distribution deals and then use them to guarantee financing.

Distribution couldn't be solidified without a constellation of stars, and so, at various times, Stephen Boyd (who was Euan's business partner), Charles Bronson, David Janssen, and possibly a few others were added and subtracted from the equation. The following paragraph from a July 25, 1970, letter that Euan allowed me to quote sums it up:

> At this time I am waiting for no fewer than five important groups to react on financing. They are all moving to a head simultaneously and I am sure two or more will jell at the same time. But that is the kind of problem that I like to face. The disappointments, the frustrations and the anger of recent months will all fade when the deal is finally closed and we are rolling forward. What a dreadful state the industry is in just now!!!

Though I believe Euan had been at the Cannes Film Festival that spring, I have no clue what, specifically, "the disappointments, the frustrations and the anger" were. But the movie business hands these out like party favors. From financial deals calculated to keep you over a barrel, to the common struggle with screenwriter after screenwriter to get an even halfway decent script, a producer's lot is much like that of a punching bag. It often seems that though there are any number of people ready to help you make your movie, all of them are also trying to destroy it in their own very personal way.

It is clear that the script was still evolving, because a short time later Louis was approached with this request:

> We also need your advice on Stage hold-ups. We need one to show how Catlow escapes from Ben in one sequence. It should be ingenious and if possible highly amusing. Can you help us. Maybe you know of some very daring incident or can dream up something. Please try.

It is hard to express how remarkable it is in the film industry for a producer to even discuss an element of a script with the author of the book; it is rarer still for the author to be asked for actual advice. Once a novelist sells the movie rights, his or her involvement is over. Dad used to say that it was like selling a house—you can't move out and think that you can tell the new owner how to redecorate.

But this was the Louis-Euan relationship in a nutshell. Euan needed a scene; Louis didn't ask questions about what they were doing to his story or if he could see the script so far—he just sent Euan a scene and kept on with whatever book he was writing. Here's the scene he sketched out:

```
SUGGESTION FOR STAGE HOLD-UP & ESCAPE:
            by Louis L'Amour.


   Ben Cowan has been tipped off that
a stage hold-up is to be attempted by
```

Catlow, and has arranged to surround the stage at the moment of the robbery. He wants them all, but Catlow in particular.

The stage is stopped in a cloud of dust, surrounded by Catlow and his men. Cowan descends upon them, the robbers break and run, the driver has a time controlling his horses, and in the moment of confusion Catlow is lost to view.

Instead of running as the others do, and knowing Ben Cowan he knows Cowan will have planned for that, he simply gets into the stage, yells to the driver to get going before somebody gets hurt and sits down gun in hand.

It is perhaps better that we simply cut from the confusion outside to the stage rolling away, then Catlow inside, smiling and holding a pistol. All have been surprised as this action is the last to be expected.

One of the lady passengers has a basket-lunch, Catlow remarks that he hasn't eaten, and suggests it be opened. With elaborate courtesy, he helps to pass out the sandwiches, chicken legs, etc., sharing with the other passengers. There is a bottle of wine, also, and they drink this.

Catlow accepts a cigar, taking it from a passenger's pocket with the

same elaborate politeness, puts another of the cigars in the passenger's mouth, and lights them both.

He rides along until reaching a
convenient spot (near where the outlaws have left an exchange of horses
or some friendly ranch) where he dis-
mounts from the stage. As he is about
to leave, and almost as an after-
thought (which it isn't) he suggests
the stage driver throw down the express box which he was after in the
first place.

The stage rolls on, he mounts a
waiting horse and rides away.

Ultimately, a different stage sequence was used; I
suspect it was a bit shorter and fit more easily into the
flow of the script. Again, this was not the sort of thing
that worried my father. He had done "his" version,
which was the book. He was willing to help his friend
out but, in the end, didn't really care what was done.
He knew that the quality of any movie was a crap-
shoot and that he wasn't even the one rolling the dice.

By January of 1971, Euan still had not been able
to get either distribution or financing in place. He
was, however, able to find a home for the film at
MGM. It was as much a way out as it was a way forward. Judging by how he spoke about it, the contract
stripped him of a good deal of the profits, if there
eventually were any, and he found it difficult to get
reimbursed for expenses he had already accrued.

On the positive side, they rapidly locked in Yul

Brynner, and by March had Leonard Nimoy and Richard Crenna. Here's what Louis wrote in his journal the morning before his first meeting with Crenna:

```
Lunch today with Sam W. [Sam Wana-
maker, the director] and Dick Crenna,
who will play Cowan. Crenna is un-
known to me personally but I've seen
him many times in films. He's good,
competent and seems to have a brain.
I will enjoy meeting him.
```

It was the beginning of a lifelong friendship. Mom and Dad at one time had a number of friends who were performers of various sorts, but by the 1970s those friendships had dwindled to a select few. Over the next few years we discovered that Richard Crenna, his wife, and his children were some of the nicest and most straightforward people we'd ever met.

As of October 1971, *Catlow* was finished and Euan, always alert to any way to attract the best publicity, arranged for it to open in Houston, Texas: a city quite taken with Hollywood glamour but off the beaten track when it came to movie premieres. This meant Houston would take the opportunity to host a premiere very seriously—exactly as Euan had planned. It goes almost without saying that Texas really knows how to throw a party. Here's how Louis described the event in his journal:

```
Opened the show in four theaters on
same night. We had limousines, one
for the MGM officials, one for Euan,
```

```
Pat [Patricia Lloyd, Euan's wife],
Kathy and I, another for Crenna and
his wife Penny, and the last for Yul
and his new bride [Jacqueline]. We
raced to the theaters with a motor-
cycle escort, appeared briefly . . .
each said a few words, Crenna did it
easiest and best, then on to the next
theater.
```

Of course I, a ten-year-old, wasn't there. I was safely in my bed back in Los Angeles. But the story goes that Crenna, always a most generous showman, took great relish in working up the Texas audience for his introduction of Brynner. Finally, he announced, "YOU-all Brynner," a pun that did not fail to bring down the house!

My father concluded his description of the evening by writing:

```
We had cocktail parties before and
after but the Crennas slipped away with
us for dinner in the hotel dining room.
```

And right there is the best part of the entire situation. Movie projects come and go, money gets made and spent, but friendships can last a lifetime. A close and long-lasting friendship with Euan led to a great and long-lasting friendship with the Crenna family.

Beau L'Amour
May 2018

# About Louis L'Amour

*"I think of myself in the oral tradition—
as a troubadour, a village taleteller, the man
in the shadows of the campfire. That's the way
I'd like to be remembered—as a storyteller.
A good storyteller."*

IT IS DOUBTFUL that any author could be as at home in the world re-created in his novels as Louis Dearborn L'Amour. Not only could he physically fill the boots of the rugged characters he wrote about, but he literally "walked the land my characters walk." His personal experiences as well as his lifelong devotion to historical research combined to give Mr. L'Amour the unique knowledge and understanding of people, events, and the challenge of the American frontier that became the hallmarks of his popularity.

As a boy growing up in Jamestown, North Dakota, he absorbed all he could about his family's frontier heritage, including the story of his great-grandfather who was scalped by Sioux warriors.

Spurred by an eager curiosity and desire to broaden his horizons, Mr. L'Amour left home at the age of fifteen and enjoyed a wide variety of jobs, including seaman, lumberjack, elephant handler, skinner of dead cattle, miner, and an officer in the transportation corps during World War II. He was a voracious reader and collector of books. His personal library contained 17,000 volumes.

Mr. L'Amour "wanted to write almost from the time I could talk." After developing a widespread following for his many frontier and adventure stories written for fiction magazines, Mr. L'Amour published his first full-length novel, *Hondo,* in the United States in 1953. Every one of his more than 120 books is in print; there are more than 300 million copies of his books in print worldwide, making him one of the bestselling authors in modern literary history. His books have been translated into twenty languages, and more than forty-five of his novels and stories have been made into feature films and television movies.

His hardcover bestsellers include *The Lonesome Gods, The Walking Drum* (his twelfth-century historical novel), *Jubal Sackett, Last of the Breed,* and *The Haunted Mesa.* His memoir, *Education of a Wandering Man,* was a leading bestseller in 1989. Audio dramatizations and adaptations of many L'Amour stories are available from Random House Audio.

The recipient of many great honors and awards, in 1983 Mr. L'Amour became the first novelist ever to be awarded the Congressional Gold Medal by the United States Congress in honor of his life's work. In 1984 he was also awarded the Medal of Freedom by President Reagan.

Louis L'Amour died on June 10, 1988.